I0773296
@fall
out
bryan

Blood in the Tea Leaves

BEKA WESTRUP

First published in the United States of America February 2023 by Beka Westrup

Cataloging-in-Publication Data is on file with the Library of Congress.

ISBN 979-8-9863087-1-5 (paperback) 979-8-9863087-0-8 (e-book)

Author website: https://www.bekawestrup.com

Editor: Borbola Branch

Cover Design: Beautiful Book Covers by Ivy

Interior Art: Bryan Camargo (@falloutbryan)

AUTHOR'S NOTE

Blood in the Tea Leaves is a spicy WLW romance, and is intended only for mature audiences. In addition to graphic sexual content, this novella addresses traumas that may be sensitive to some readers.

A list of content warnings has been provided below.

Please take care.

- Explicit Sexual Content
- Blood
- Death/Murder
- Theme of/References to Child Death
- Kidnapping of a Child
- Mention of Rape

Also: this is a prequel novella that may be read as a standalone. However, I highly recommend reading it after Beneath the Bloody Aurora, as this story has some time jumps that are informed by BTBA.

PLAYLIST

~

1. Ivy by Taylor Swift

2. Control by Zoe Wees

3. A Sky Full of Stars by Coldplay

4. High Infidelity by Taylor Swift

5. I Feel It in The Wind by Smith and Thell

6. Wake Me Up (feat. Fleurie) by Tommy Profitt

7. mad woman by Taylor Swift

8. You'd Never Know by BLÜ EYES

9. The Great War by Taylor Swift

10. Let You Know by Sody

11. You're On Your Own, Kid by Taylor Swift

For women.
God, I love women.

PART I

THE TURN

MARIE

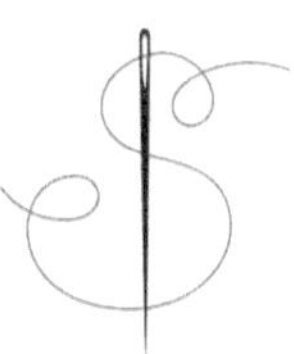

Marie had grown well-acquainted with the sharpest agonies in life, but pricking her fingertip on her sewing needle was a blow that hit harder than most, for she had done it to herself.

She hissed, lifting her hand to examine the damage.

The cut welled and oozed a droplet the darkest shade of red, the puncture deeper than she expected. Before the blood had a chance to fall and ruin her work, she popped her finger into her mouth, spreading the copper tang across her tongue. By the time she withdrew her finger, the skin was already sealing back together. The needle left behind only the faintest pinprick of pink.

She stood in front of a dress form, stitching floral embroidery on the powder-blue gown she'd been laboring over for the last five days. She hadn't left the shop since the order came in.

Her mentor—the owner of this shop and one the most esteemed Ladies on this side of the country—told her it was a customer of great importance, and Marie was able to convince her husband to let her stay in the shop overnight to complete the dress before Sunday, when the shop would close and the post would be sent out.

Four nights now, she'd managed to avoid him. It was a brief but heavenly reprieve from home, but she knew it wouldn't last much longer.

He'd come searching for her soon. He'd drag her back home and demand the things from her that he always did. Suppers that he would eventually throw up in a drunken stupor. Her body in their lumpy bed. Her screams, if he was angry enough.

It doesn't matter, she told herself.

Four nights of peace was nothing short of a miracle, and she knew when to thank the Light for its mercy. She knew when not to ask for too much.

She was practically finished with the dress now, only a few more stitches and one last look-over. Marie hoped the customer this was headed to would love it, hoped they would tell their friends and send more business.

Additional business meant more late nights in this cove of peace she'd carved for herself, surrounded by quiet and color and soft material. More time holding her needle, which felt so much like her only weapon these days, she often considered carrying it home. Perhaps she should. She wanted to so badly sometimes, her whole body ached with the urge… but she could never quite muster the courage to follow through.

Smiling at the pink flower between her fingers, she tied off her thread. Then she took a step back and admired the work in its entirety.

The material gleamed in the candlelight of the back room,

where the shop's windows were shuttered to preserve the finery. Marie inched toward the candle burning beside her and set her needle down for the first time in hours. She stared at the flame. Now that she was finished with her work, her attention was drawn to every hurt in her body. She had lost track of time. Her eyes were heavy, and growing heavier by the moment. Her stomach growled.

Without looking toward the front room, she could tell it was nearing late afternoon.

Marie wasn't sure how long she stood there, swaying with exhaustion, staring at the candle. She was immobilized by the cold dread spreading through her belly at the prospect of leaving this place, of returning to a shack that did not feel like home.

And then the door to the shop opened.

Marie straightened. Her fingers grazed the discarded needle, but she hesitated as the door swung shut and she heard the lock flip. Gentle footsteps padded across the front room.

She recognized the light, measured gait, and a smile sprung to her lips. Her stomach filled with a searing warmth that chased away her fears.

Those footsteps grew louder, clicking against the wooden floor as her visitor entered the back room, and onward they clicked until heat encroached on her spine. A breath caressing her neck. Delicate fingers sweeping her curtain of blonde hair to one shoulder. A kiss pressed to her collar.

Her eyes fluttered shut.

Marie melted into the soft body behind her. Another kiss emblazoned her neck like a brand, teeth grazing the tender skin beneath her ear. A dulcet voice whispered in her ear, "My love."

She twisted and met those warm lips with a kiss of her own, wrapping her arms around petite shoulders, threading her fingers into a pile of messy yellow hair. She didn't close her eyes, couldn't. Not when it had been hours since she last looked upon Alice's face—the beautiful woman who had stolen and mended her heart.

Alice's features softened when they kissed.

The sharpness faded from her brown eyes, and the seemingly permanent crease in her forehead disappeared. The sight sent tingling heat surging through Marie's stomach, dropping to swirl in her core.

Alice returned the kiss eagerly, bracketing her hands on Marie's waist and pulling her closer. She seemed to attempt to keep her eyes open, understanding the open gaze of intimacy Marie loved so well... but they fluttered shut as she deepened the kiss.

Her soft lips coaxed Marie's open, her tongue slipping into her mouth. Caressing, claiming, filling.

Marie let her eyes shut too and allowed the embrace to overwhelm her. Needy fingers, ragged breaths. The kiss filled her with clouds and color, with a passion greater than anything she'd ever experienced before—not even with her needle.

Marie loved her work, but she loved Alice more.

Just when she thought they might move to the chaise nearby—the way they always did when their bodies ran hot and their time ran short—Alice pulled away.

Alice laughed at Marie's pout, threading fingers into her curls as she said quietly, "I didn't know if you would still be here."

Marie stepped back with a grimace, kissing the palm of

Alice's hand before turning away to clean up the room. Alice wanted to *talk*. And it was so exhausting for Marie to talk about going back home. "I just barely finished the dress," she explained. "And Lady Colette made a day trip to the city, so I'll have to stay at least until the shop closes for the night."

The room fell silent as Marie finished stowing her tools, but she felt Alice's eyes on her. She sensed how much Alice kept to herself. Their situation was irremediable, and they both knew it.

Marie was mere property to be moved around and used however her husband saw fit. It didn't bother her to think of her life in realistic terms—there was no other way to survive. Before her husband, she had belonged to her father, who made it clear what he thought of her when he sold her for a stack of gold pieces. Not a tall stack, either. She doubted what her husband paid for her had even been enough to get the family through the following winter. But she'd been the oldest of five. Marrying her off was a relief to her parents. They didn't care if it made her hate her life so much more than when she'd just been a starving, and often forgotten, daughter.

Alice was traditionally unattached—but just as trapped. Her profession as a prostitute didn't exactly lend her the ability to live a life free of men. They still owned her, for minutes at a time.

In a lot of ways, Marie felt as though their suffering was equal. Even the pains they did not speak aloud bonded them. They understood each other because they felt the same agony —being a woman in a world that only valued men. Being a woman when happiness seemed to rely so heavily on how much power you held over others. Marie and Alice did what-ever they had to in order to be together. They skirted around the miserable truths that kept them apart and pretended that what they shared could last forever.

Alice broke the silence with a scoff and ambled towards her. "The shop is already closed," she said coyly.

She halted behind Marie, almost pressed up against her back, but not quite. Marie felt her begin to play with her hair, even while no other part of them touched, even while she *yearned*. That was the way Alice seduced her… relentless coaxing disguised as innocent touches. She'd be lying if she said she didn't like it. *Love* it.

"It's getting late," Marie whispered.

"The sun is still shining," Alice replied easily, trailing her fingertips down Marie's spine until she found the laces of her dress. She started loosening them.

Marie's lips parted, common sense on the tip of her tongue, but her breath was already quickening.

This was the understanding between them; the days were theirs, and the days were safe. And as long as the sun was shining, they could find each other in the shadows. It wasn't enough for Marie—loving with her whole heart, only half of the time—but this thing between them was still her *everything*. The only thing that mattered.

Alice drew her dress open, dragged the sides off her shoulders and let it pool around her ankles.

Marie's flesh prickled, her nipples hardening and beginning to ache as her head fell to the side. She silently begged for Alice to warm her skin with kisses. But of course she didn't. She wasn't done teasing.

Alice turned Marie so they were facing each other, and when Marie swayed forward to close the space between them, Alice kept her at bay with a gentle but firm grip on her upper arms. Marie continued to lean in, pushing against Alice's hold, her chest expanding in great gasps. Alice surveyed the length of her body. And Marie loved it when Alice looked at her like that. Like she was beautiful. Like she was special. Like she was... perfect.

Alice took a small step forward, drawing so close, it was as good as an embrace, and brushed her mouth against Marie's. Not a real kiss. *Not enough.*

A moan tore from Marie's throat, low and flustered. Her hands grappled with Alice's wrists as she attempted to dislodge them, but before she could get an advantage and free herself, Alice broke off the kiss.

She smirked, her eyes warm. Love drunk. "Hmm," she hummed, pressing another kiss to the corner of Marie's mouth, another to her cheek. Her jaw. Her neck. "Even after all this time, you're still so impatient."

"It's not my fault you set me on fire," Marie murmured, not even knowing her own thoughts before she said them. "I feel like I'm burning alive when I look at you."

Alice's breath caught, and the reaction lit a flame in Marie so hot, she felt herself melt. If not for Alice's hold on her arms, her knees might have buckled.

Alice composed herself in the next heartbeat, chuckling into Marie's ear. "You don't burn alone." But even as she said it, she pulled away. She released Marie's arms and glided to the center of the room where the dress form was.

"Alice," Marie breathed, desperation hitching her voice.

Alice ignored her, a smile playing on her lips as she stopped in front of the finished dress. Marie swayed where Alice abandoned her, utterly naked, feeling exposed and the tiniest bit jilted. Her heart pounded against her ribs. If Alice didn't touch her soon, she was going to snap. But then, Alice liked her like that—driven mad with need, teased until she just couldn't stand it. Marie was tested until she *took* what she wanted.

And she knew Alice liked being on the receiving end of her frustrations a little too much. It had developed into an addiction for them of the most dangerous sort.

Alice caressed the square collar of the dress. "You've created a masterpiece, Marie." She was up to something, Marie just wasn't sure what.

"Thank you." Marie's words were almost inaudible.

Alice leered at Marie, that smile of hers growing. "Try it on."

Blinking, Marie repeated that request in her mind. Her skin prickled. She glanced at the dress, considering it, knowing it would fit. She shook her head and wrapped her arms around her torso, a shield against the dusky air suddenly seeping into the shop. "I can't."

Alice tilted her head. "Why not?"

There were about a dozen different reasons not to, the most obvious one being that it was perhaps the most expensive dress she'd ever made. Marie's entire wardrobe amounted to nothing in comparison.

"It's a Lady's gown," she said.

Alice's eyes flashed with anger. Not anger with Marie, of course—Alice was never angry with her. Her jaw clenched, one of her eyebrows piquing as she folded her arms under her breasts.

"Come here," she commanded, her voice dark and entirely irresistible. Marie had *never* been able to resist her.

Marie met Alice in the center of the room.

Alice turned her attention to the dress, unbuttoning the back and pulling it off the form with painstaking gentleness. The reverence Alice showed for Marie's work stole her breath away, and any further objection was forgotten as Alice returned to her side to whisper in her ear, "You deserve to be clothed in silk and diamonds, Marie. Your soul sparkles brighter than the stars."

Alice dressed her, and Marie's chest filled with the tender sensation of being cared for. She'd prayed for that so often as a child, it triggered a soreness in her heart.

None of this was real. She would never own a gown like this. She would never be with Alice the way she truly wanted. For whatever reason, the Divine Light did not deem her worthy of it. *She* was not worthy, and she remembered that every time Alice told her the opposite.

She'd been told the truth since infancy, when she was a sickly babe that wore on her mother's nerves. And again, when every labor around her parents' farm caused her sickness and injury, when she turned into more of a burden than even her youngest siblings. They told her it was her fault. She earned her frailness, her sickliness, her bruises and neglect. No one ever told her *how* she earned it, only that the Divine Light did not make mistakes. She'd offended their god, somehow, and it was punishing her.

Her whole youth, she'd sought forgiveness. Now, she was almost certain her offense was being born in the first place. Her existence was the sin. So what use was it to pray?

By the time Alice finished buttoning the dress, Marie was choking back tears. She bit her lip so hard, she tasted copper as she tried to hide it. But as Alice nuzzled the nape of her neck, as she slipped her arms around Marie's waist and hugged her tightly, the sobs were noticed.

Alice peered over Marie's shoulder and cupped her cheek to force her to look up. "What is it? What's wrong?"

Marie shook her head. She was beyond words. Hot tears streaked her face as she shut her eyes in shame. They had such little time together already, and now she was wasting it.

Alice sighed, her exhale washing over Marie with the scent of mint leaf and a hint of the alcohol she no doubt washed her mouth with before leaving the brothel. The reminder only made Marie weep harder. Alice tugged her close, petting her hair, whispering sweet nothings in her ear until the heaviness passed. She knew Alice would hold her the whole night this way if she needed it.

"I'm sorry, I didn't mean to cry," Marie finally muttered. "I didn't want to do this to you."

Alice lifted Marie's chin, looking into her eyes as she said, "Do what? I love you when you laugh, and when you cry. Whatever you need—whatever time or affection or space—I will give it to you. It's all right to be yourself with me."

Those words soothed a raw wound inside her. It *was* all right. *This* was right, the two of them.

Marie felt the heat rekindle in her belly, violent lust enveloping her body in a hailstorm of brilliance. She fell forward and captured Alice's lips with her own.

Everything that followed was as effortless as breathing.

One kiss led to another as they stumbled across the room. Tiny, pulsing thrills chased up Marie's spine and she sensed Alice holding back, those desperate hands treading the line between delicate and bestial as they skimmed her curves. She was trying to preserve the dress. Marie found that incredibly sweet, but she didn't care much about the dress right now. She wouldn't have blinked if Alice tore it off her body.

Alice's slight figure pressed Marie down into the chaise.

A moan rose unbidden from Marie's throat. There was no light or surrounding, no sense of time outside the shop. There was nothing but Alice. Her sweet fingers knotting in Marie's hair. The softness of Alice's mouth. The slick caress of her tongue and the arch of her Cupid's bow. The scrape of teeth and the throb of their swelling lips.

"Let me make you feel good," Alice said against her mouth.

Marie didn't object, could barely think of anything beyond the warmth in her body as Alice pulled back and started hitching the dress up her legs. Nails grazed her inner thighs, drawing lines toward her center, and her hips twitched without permission.

Alice withdrew her touch before her hands could rise any higher, laughing as she settled between Marie's legs. She spread Marie wider, pressing kisses to the inside of her knee. Then she moved to the other leg. Kissed higher. She moved methodically, touching every sensitive spot as though she'd mapped them out in her head and wanted to remind herself of the journey.

By the time Marie felt Alice's breath caress her core, she was thoroughly soaked and writhing.

Alice pushed the bottom of the dress up to gather over her stomach, but then she paused, staring with a furrowed brow at the hem as she lifted it.

"What is this?"

In her hand, she held the letters Marie had embroidered into the dress. Marie didn't know enough of her letters to read

—her Lady was still in the process of teaching her—but she knew what letters Alice and her own name started with. That was enough to start leaving these marks on each of her gowns. It was an M, sewn with a subtle white thread, with the first arch of the letter crossed to appear like an A.

The two of them, together… in every way she could manage.

Alice saw what she had done, and her eyes filled with tears, even as a smile bloomed. "My love, why would you…?" Her voice broke.

Marie said, "You fill my heart and my thoughts. You are already in every stitch."

Rubbing her wet eyes, Alice nodded. But before she could continue where they left off, her gaze caught on a gap in the hem a few inches away from the lettering. "Oh, but look. You forgot this portion."

Marie shook her head. "Colette prefers that I let her finish each dress so she can check over my work. Especially the ones that are this expensive."

Though, Marie suspected that her Lady's request went beyond a desire to inspect her work. She'd walked in on too many whispered conversations by now, had seen the strange items that often came into the shop only to promptly disappear. Marie noticed how the weight of some dresses she made changed after her Lady put her hands on them. But she would not say a word about that.

Alice didn't reply, only frowned and scooted back on the chaise.

There was an obvious tension between Alice and their town's Lady, an unease that permeated the room whenever all three of them were together. It had grown to the point where Alice was bothered by the mere mention of her.

Marie wished she knew the source so she could make it right. They were the two most important people in her life, but neither woman seemed willing to have a conversation about their differences, not with each other as far as she knew, and certainly not with her.

Alice shook free of her frown, pointedly changing the subject. "I brought something for us to play with."

She stood from the chaise and walked to the leather bag she'd left under the archway into the room. Marie leaned up on her elbows as Alice dug through the contents and quietly withdrew something. As she turned back to face her, Marie's stomach dipped.

"What is that?"

Alice smiled, caressing the cylinder of pleated leather in her hands. "What does it look like?"

Marie grimaced. "Like my nightmares." She recognized the shape and could guess its purpose. She'd been avoiding home for the same reason she frowned at the item in Alice's fingers. She knew how much it hurt.

"Don't worry," Alice said quickly, as if that would lighten Marie's darkening thoughts, "it's new." She glided closer, and Marie inched back on the chaise.

Swallowing the dread in her throat, Marie tried to keep her voice steady as she said, "I—I don't know, Alice. I don't think this is a good idea."

"Why not?" Alice spoke with genuine curiosity. There was no hint of malice, no impatience. She seemed to understand that Marie had started spiraling inwardly because she simply perched on the far side of the chaise as she waited for an answer.

Marie drew her knees to her chest. "I just…I don't think I would enjoy it."

Alice considered that for a moment. She set aside the leather column, hitched her dress, and crawled over the seat to Marie. Her eyes were soft. Her smile small, but sure. When her chest was nearly touching Marie's knees, she reached up and tugged on Marie's wrists.

She drew Marie's hands up to her face. Then Alice grazed her hands across Marie's shins, slipping them between her thighs and gently opening her up. The whole time, Alice looked into Marie's eyes, holding her captive, stoking those flickers of warmth back into a blaze.

When Marie was spread, her arousal glistened like a silent plea between them. Alice answered it with gentle, eager fingers, and there was no possibility of resisting then.

Marie's head rocked back against the chaise, her legs falling open and her body going molten in all the right places. Every stroke was intentional. Every stroke mattered. They sent rolling sparks fluttering under her skin, right down to her toes.

Her eyes slid closed, but she still heard Alice whisper, "Don't you want to feel me deep inside you, Marie? I'll claim every inch. Every time that monster touches you, you won't be able to think of anything but me."

Alice's hand shifted lower, even while she kept her thumb brushing that sensitive bud. She kept the thrust of her fingers shallow. Slow and hard. Teasing so viciously, Marie forgot what she was worried over in the first place.

"I already think of you," she breathed.

"Not like this." There was a smile in Alice's voice now. Alice slid her fingers in a little deeper. She kissed Marie's soft, lean belly. "I'll put my mark on your body, my love, and it will remember me. I'll be sealed permanently beneath your skin."

Marie moaned. "*Yes.*"

The air in the room fizzled, an invisible weight, a blanket of heat that tickled her skin as Alice arranged herself back between her legs. "We can stop at any moment," Alice swore, her lips brushing Marie's center. "Just say the word."

Alice didn't immediately pick up the leather prop as Marie expected, but rather tended to her throbbing ache with tongue and teeth. With dextrous fingers and rumbling moans. It was only when Marie rose to a luminous peak that she felt Alice remove her mouth. It was almost painful, retreating sharply from her pleasure. But then she glanced down and saw Alice sucking on the column of leather, her hazel eyes trained on Marie's face.

It shouldn't have sent a fresh thrill coursing down her spine, but that *look*.

Without a word, Alice returned her mouth to Marie's center. Sensation overwhelmed her. That peak reappeared, her body building toward it with urgency, even as the smooth head of leather prodded at her opening. There was only one moment of uncertainty, where her breath caught and her body tightened, and Alice paused, working the bud with renewed agency, broad strokes followed by delicate swirls. Marie melted once again.

Slowly, it pushed into her.

She was surprised by how easy it felt, how painless. Her back started arching in need, aching for the intrusion, for *more*. Alice obliged her. In and in, until Marie was gasping around the fullness.

"You're doing so well," Alice murmured between kisses.

Alice withdrew, then pushed back in. And it became a song, a melody between them. The rhythm of Alice's hands and tongue, and the need building in Marie's body with vicious shudders. The flames in her tummy raged on, crackling, *all-consuming*. She wanted to tell Alice that she was right, that this was what she wanted after all.

All Marie could manage was another drawn-out moan.

"Can you feel me? I'm deeper now than he's ever been." There was amusement in Alice's voice, delight. But there was a darkness too, a primal yearning they both knew only Marie could satiate. "And you love it. I'm the only one who can make you feel like this."

Marie wasn't sure why that made her stomach tighten, why it made every inch of her skin prickle as she finally touched that bright precipice and balanced on its edge.

"Alice," Marie gasped, reaching blindly for her. "Kiss me."

Alice leaned up, replacing her tongue with the fingers of her free hand and continuing to drive that leather in and out of Marie's core as their lips met. Marie thought it tasted like salt and sin. Nothing this good, this delicious, could ever lead to heaven. So she would happily burn.

"That's it," Alice purred. "Burst for me, my love."

Marie did. She fell into the unfathomable heat that she'd recently become so used to in Alice's arms, her vision swirling with dark stars and her body clamping around that hard column, the intrusion spurring her pleasure on and on. She admitted to herself that she could get used to *that*.

When it was over, Alice pulled the leather tool from her and stood from the chaise.

Marie kept her eyes closed, her bones sinking into the cushions beneath her. She heard the rustling of material and then Alice saying, "Lift your arms, love."

Alice helped her out of the dress.

Marie watched as she gathered it up and draped it over the form, treating it with so much care that Marie's chest clenched all over again. Then Alice removed her own clothes and returned to the chaise. Alice smiled, almost shyly, and stretched out on top of Marie.

Marie shuddered at the warmth, holding Alice as they went boneless together. They didn't say anything for several long moments. Alice only rested a cheek against Marie's breast. Marie caressed slow loops across her back.

Until Alice said quietly, "Sometimes, I wish we were men."

Marie's fingers froze. She looked down at Alice, her brows furrowing. "Why?"

Alice sighed, trailing her fingertips up Marie's side. "Then we could run away together and no one would care. No one would come after us."

Marie saw the pain in her eyes then—that pain she so often kept hidden.

It was a useless wish, but Marie understood. The desire had crossed her mind once or twice, to run away. To *try*. But they couldn't, they would never succeed. Even if Marie's husband didn't come after them—if he somehow decided that the effort of finding and retrieving her outweighed the benefit, which was unlikely considering how much money her work now brought in—then they still had Alice's madame to think about. Alice was indebted to her brothel. She was an asset, and they would never allow her to get away.

Marie smiled sadly and tucked a lock of Alice's yellow hair behind her ear. "I don't."

"No?" Alice's eyes were wide, vulnerable.

"No. I don't wish you were a man." Marie shifted so that they lay side-by-side, and slowly wiggled her way down the chaise, pressing kisses to Alice's skin as she went. "*This* is so much better."

Marie resorted to distraction because what else could she do?

Alice raked in a great breath as Marie found her target and began returning every ounce of pleasure she'd received. Marie savored the taste of hell and pretended for a little while longer… that these stolen moments could last forever.

COLETTE

Lady Colette Valand rode her mare into the city twice a year. Once in the spring for market, when seeds and new fabrics could be found in abundant supply, and once in the fall for pleasure, before the long winter kept her contained to the small town in which she lived.

She was returning home from one of her fall excursions when a man waved her down just outside of town.

Colette curled her lip in annoyance and reluctantly let go of her skirts, allowing them tumble down from where she held them on top of her bare, plump thighs. Her mare had been galloping on and off for the last hour; too much heat radiated from it for her to remain modest. Not that she cared much about modesty, even when other people were around to admire her.

But she wasn't in her home right now. She wasn't with her oblivious husband or her friends or the carefully selected male guests that came to visit her expecting such impropriety. This was the greater town. Her neighbors. And that man approaching her was perhaps the only neighbor she was not fond of at all.

Marie's husband, Henri.

Colette took Marie under her wing after the couple moved in from a nearby province. She had hardly laid eyes on Marie when she first knocked on the Bernards' door, but the gossip about them spread like wildfire after only their first month in town—the whispers that Henri beat his wife. Her screams were heard by the neighboring farms and every detail relayed to Colette.

She'd offered Marie a job in her shop the very next day.

Marie learned to sew under Colette's close tutelage, and the fragile flower *bloomed*. She became the busiest seamstress for miles and gained a hesitant, grateful pride… but the farms and Colette knew what happened when she returned home. When night fell, suffering echoed from that shack on the outskirts of town.

Colette longed for the day when it would not go ignored.

When Henri got within arm's reach, she halted her mare. The miserable stench of gin and sweat wafted up to her as he slurred, "Where is my wife?"

She replied tartly, "Henri, you know she is working."

Henri smiled tightly, a foul gleam in his eye. "I would not bother my Lady if that was the case. Alas, I have just been by the shop and found it closed for the day."

Colette looked to the horizon and shook her head. "You're mistaken. The shop should be open for an hour yet."

He made a low noise that might have been a scoff and gestured down the road into town. "Walk with me, and I'll show you."

A shiver rolled down Colette's spine. She grazed a hand

over the dagger strapped to her thigh. She was rarely afraid of men. On the contrary, over the course of her marriage, she'd welcomed plenty of quiet affairs, considering her husband was too decrepit to notice or try to please her himself. He was sixty when she married him. She gave him four strapping boys, and that was quite enough to appease him and the responsibility they shared to his family's name.

On the rare occasion, if she engaged with a man who made her feel like this—uneasy and a little bit frightened—she didn't hesitate to pull the knife from her thigh.

She didn't pull that blade now. She only nodded and allowed Henri to walk ahead.

As they made their way into town, Colette kept her distance from him. He was drunk and unbalanced, more than usual, and his hands kept fisting at his sides. He was angry. She felt it like a storm cloud looming on the horizon. Cruelty radiated from his pores along with the alcohol, attacking her senses like barbs being kicked up from the road.

When they reached the shop, Colette realized Henri was telling the truth.

The shop was dark.

With twilight fast approaching, she dismounted and fished around in her pouch to retrieve her key for the bronze, aging lock. Henri stood behind her, the stench of him hitting her anew as she fumbled with the door. He was breathing erratically, heavily. The hair on the nape of her neck stood up straight. His drunken gasps reminded her of her husband when she'd been forced to attend to him as a younger woman. Her uncle who had constantly sniffed around her when she was still a girl. Men who walked a little too close to death, but never had the decency to submit to it. Unhappy men. The Living Dead.

A small voice in the back of her head told her to spin around and slam the key into his neck.

The instant the lock clicked free, Henri shoved past her into the shop.

She cried out as they tumbled over the threshold and his silhouette barreled toward the back room. Colette knew when he pushed past the curtains, when she heard the girlish shrieks and his face turned red as a beet, that everything was about to change.

"You whore," Henri roared. "You answered the call of the void, have you? You wish to die?"

Colette squared her shoulders and threw herself into the storm.

"What's the meaning of this," she commanded, elbowing her way into the back room. She positioned herself between Henri and his wife, and forced a gasp of outrage when she saw Marie tangled up with another woman on the settee.

Colette launched into a prayer to the Divine Light, speaking loud enough for her voice to bounce off the walls of the room.

Marie was frozen on the chaise, her eyes wide and welling with fearful tears, her long flaxen curls mussed. The other woman pulled on her clothes with trained efficiency.

"A prostitute," Henri growled over Colette's prayer. He took a lumbering step, leering at Alice's garters, vengeance in his eyes. And Colette's heart took off in a thundering beat. "That's how you spend our money?"

Marie shook her head, tears spilling over. She stood on unsteady legs.

Colette strode across the room, cutting off Henri's advance and slapped her protégée in the face.

The prostitute started, but Colette pinned her with a vicious look. Marie wept openly as Colette said to her, "This is treacherous, my girl. You should be ashamed of yourself. In my shop no less, after all I've done for you? Cover yourself this instant."

Marie knelt to gather her clothes.

Colette turned to the prostitute. "And you," she hissed, a layer of warning in her eyes. "Your Madame will be hearing about *this*."

Marie, who had just slipped her dress up over her shoulders, startled as her husband interjected to say, "Make haste, woman. I'm taking you home."

The words were laced with the silkiest venom, and anyone in the world would have heard it—the promise of what was to come.

Colette rose to her full posture and turned on her heel to face Henri. She plastered a sweet, sympathetic smile on her face and crooned, "Henri, you poor dear, go home and rest your tired heart. Should The Divine Light will it, I would like to sit with Marie for an hour and give her a proper sermon on what it means to be a good wife. Then, I will send her home to repent to you."

The entire room stilled, passion and duty swirling between them. Henri's face darkened. His hands fisted again, but there was nothing for him to hold on to.

No one would dare deny a Lady's request, not even the town drunk.

"May The Light guide you," he muttered. Henri looked to his wife, but he had no words for her. He glared at the prostitute and spat, dispersing his hatred across her chest before retreating back through the shop, slamming the door as he left.

Colette rushed to the door and locked it, watching through the window as he veered in the direction of the tavern. She took a deep breath, willing her nerves to calm. Then she searched for a candle. The sun was finally beyond the horizon, and night would soon envelop them.

When she finally made it back to the room, Marie's sobs had ebbed, but she remained rooted to the settee. Her dress was unbuttoned in the back, forgotten entirely as she stared at the dwindling candle on the side table.

She whispered, "What shall I do?"

Alice sidled up next to Marie and embraced her. By the candlelight, Colette watched as Alice wiped away Marie's tears, fastened the dress, and spoke gentle comforts in her ear. Marie reached up and clung to Alice's sleeves, staring into her eyes as if anchoring herself there, as if it was Alice alone who kept her from collapsing into dust.

A strike of lightning. That was what it had been for those two.

An affair that was more than just an affair, an intimacy so permanent and bone-deep, they risked everything in the pursuit of being together. Colette had warned Marie many times how dangerous it was to continue this, to love so completely when it would only end in pain. Marie had already suffered enough pain for a lifetime. A thousand lifetimes.

Colette had yet to experience such a metamorphosis of the heart and wagered she never, ever would.

Marie had once tried to explain it. "*My blood called to hers, and it would not stop singing.*" Colette couldn't hear the music, but she could see the dance. She would sometimes find her toes tapping to their rhythm, find herself aching to understand. She would sometimes watch them without meaning to, mesmerized, the way she was doing now.

Alice smoothed Marie's curls, kissing the cheek that was raised and rouge.

Colette couldn't bear it, the sadness and craving she so often felt around them. Shattering the serenity, she said, "You girls have done it now."

The prostitute turned to Colette, her face guttering with flame and shadow, all tenderness dissolving into ire as she growled, "You *hit* her."

"Don't be a fool," Colette replied, lifting her chin. "I saved her."

"It won't last," Marie said emptily. "He will come for me when I do not return home. He will punish me. He will kill me this time, I'm sure of it."

Alice began to vibrate with unadulterated fury.

Colette's heart burned and twisted to think of what Marie would face when she returned to her husband. The husband she hated. The husband who had never deserved her.

Lady Colette Valand kept innumerable secrets in her life, had prided herself on her unfaltering discretion… but that day, she let her mouth open for the sake of what she saw between the women before her. "Then I suppose, dearests, we must make you disappear."

MARIE

Marie had never seen the Lady serve her own tea before, and she had to admit… it was unsettling to witness. Colette carried the tea tray into the grand salon room, having dismissed her maid for the evening, and slid the silver platter onto the table.

The room was acutely dark. Only a single candle flickered on the far end of the round table. The sitting room was too large, its ivory walls too far away to reflect that meager flame, and so the recesses of the room turned into inky pools of night, the shadows waiting on bated breath for secrets they were bound to be spilling soon.

This room was as stunning as her Lady. Pale. Soft and curved generously in all the perfect places. Flecked every-where with gold, similar to how her skin was speckled with freckles and birthmarks. Colette's sensual nature shone in every stroke of paint on the mural ceiling, and the accents of deep red in the upholstery were as vibrant as her hair, strik-ingly so.

Marie had been here only a handful of times, fewer still when the chandeliers were fully lit and one of her parties were roaring. Each time, she was astounded by how blatantly Colette's husband showed his admiration.

Colette set a golden-rimmed cup in front of Marie and filled it with trembling hands. Marie knew that slight tremble would be the only indication of her nerves. She was too aware of the risk they were both taking by delaying the inevitable, by hiding in this manor when Henri was impatiently waiting for her return. Every minute she spent here would make her punishment worse. And the last thing she wanted to do was drag Colette into this.

Reaching across the table, Marie touched her wrist. "Forgive me."

Porcelain clattered as Colette nearly dropped the teapot, and her gilded green eyes slid up to meet Marie's. She sighed. Then she put aside the tea pot and cradled Marie's face in both of her hands. They were warm. Few in the province believed the Lady could be warm, what with her crude humor in private and no-nonsense attitude when dealing with customers. But she often was with Marie—so very warm.

"My dear one," Colette breathed, caressing her cheeks with both thumbs, "there is nothing to forgive."

It was the most direct confession of acceptance Colette had ever voiced to her.

Grateful tears sprang to Marie's eyes, but Colette only shushed her and told her to drink some tea. It was bitter, metallic. Marie didn't care for the nobility's fascination with tea, but she continued to sip at it, simply because Colette wanted her to.

Colette smiled at her approvingly and then filled her own cup, the steam curling upward to kiss her pink cheeks.

The double doors on the opposite side of the room, the entry closest to the foyer, flew open, and Alice breezed in with a cloaked woman on her heels. Marie instantly scanned her lover's body and face, ensuring she had not been unfortunate enough to cross paths with Henri on her errand.

That's what she feared the most—more than the bedroom she shared with her husband, more than the torrent of damnation that followed her every thought. She feared for Alice, and what they both knew Henri was capable of doing to her. Prostitutes died all the time.

But Alice crossed the salon easily.

Marie slumped against her armrest in relief, and Alice slipped into the chair beside her, dragging it close enough to grip her hand beneath the table.

The cloaked woman paused on the other side of the table, facing Colette.

After a moment's hesitation, the stranger pushed back her hood.

Marie recognized her when the candles illuminated her delicate cheekbones, the sprawling black ringlets and her staggering blue eyes. It was Genevieve. She frequently saw Genevieve's small family around town. Once primed for a life of nobility, the dark-haired beauty surrendered her birthright for a love match.

She lived far more simply now, in a cottage right in the center of town, with her husband and the son they had together who regularly accompanied her on daily errands.

When working hours were over, she and her husband were seldom seen apart. Always sitting outside together or walking the town, touching and gazing, openly loving each other. It was a sight Marie couldn't understand until she met Alice. Before Alice, she did not know love could be a gentle, affectionate thing. That that was what love *should* be.

A weight plummeted in her stomach, knowing she would never have the opportunity to stroll through town with Alice that way. Knowing she might never live to see another day at all, unless Colette contrived a plan to save her. She didn't doubt for a heartbeat that Colette was capable of it.

Colette busied herself with the tea, serving her two new guests.

Genevieve eyed the tea pot, then the dim recesses of the room. "Where are your young lads?"

"My Lord has taken them on a visit to Court. He thought it would be a good opportunity for them to learn of our family's service to the King." She smiled tightly.

What was she up to?

"Which is quite alright with me," Colette added with a sharp laugh, "seeing as I get some peace and quiet out of it."

Genevieve frowned, turning her ear toward the dark corner behind her. "The shadows are charged around us. Why have you brought me here, what do you want?"

Alice squeezed Marie's hand, and she knew it was a command to keep silent. Her flesh broke out in goosebumps. The night outside the room's gilded windows suddenly seemed so much darker. Genevieve had a reputation in town of being disturbed. She listened to silence and swore she heard voices, *spirits*. It did not lend her many friends, but she rarely bothered anyone. Most of the town simply avoided her in the evening—as that seemed to be when they spoke to her most—and waved the madness off as a harmless quirk.

Whether it was indeed a quirk or something more nefarious, the reminder that those voices existed in Genevieve's head never failed to unsettle her. Marie tried not to wiggle in her chair.

Colette cleared her throat. "I'm calling in my favor."

Genevieve lifted the tea to her lips and drank, the shadows shifting behind her as she said, "I have no recollection of a debt. What favor do you speak of?"

A shrug. "The one I earned from my discretion of your personal affairs—the service you run in the darkness. I have wares that need passage."

Marie squeezed Alice's hand in return, and their eyes met. She could hardly believe it. Colette's plan became clear to her then. The smuggling channel—the rumors of which had been circulating for many months now—was real. It was real, and Colette had found it.

Genevieve leaned forward in her chair, slamming the tea cup back into its saucer as she bared her teeth and hissed, "I don't have a clue as to what you're talking about."

Colette didn't react, which was more than Marie could say about herself. Even Alice jumped a little. The Lady simply sniffed her tea before draining it in one long sip. "Genevieve, dear," she wiped away a wayward drip with her frilly sleeve, "you should know by now that I hear every going-on in our town."

Genevieve's throat bobbed, but she otherwise remained stoic.

"Did you think I would not notice when the people in my town began to disappear?" Colette mused. "When wares went missing, and my dress deliveries never made it to their destinations? Do you think I am oblivious to the company you and your husband associate with in the middle of the night?"

Alice reached for the cup in front of her, and Marie realized belatedly that it was to hide a smile. Her lover might not be especially fond of Colette, but it proved impossible not to admire her when she played her tricks.

Genevieve reclined in the chair, though every muscle in her body still seemed coiled to strike. "Are you threatening to expose us?"

Colette's smile grew, genuine and almost sadistic in its slow spread. Marie swallowed against the pulse thundering in her throat, the air filling with foreboding silence as the Lady looked around the table. Colette was playing with them like she would strings on a fiddle. If Marie wasn't so sure that whatever Colette planned to tell them would change life as they knew it, she might have laughed at her friend's theatrics.

Finally, Colette lifted her chin and said, "Why would I do that, when I am the reason it exists?"

There it was. The catalyst that succeeded in rocking Marie to her core. She couldn't breathe for a moment as reality set in. The dresses. Colette had been smuggling intel inside of them.

Genevieve's jaw slackened. She blinked once, twice. "Pardon?"

Colette shrugged. "I keep myself well-concealed. I have to. But someone had to form that initial contact, and who better to do that than the unassuming, party-loving Lady in the East. No one has ever looked twice at me. I complain about the interceptions to my deliveries loud enough to drown out their suspicions, look down my nose at those vying for war, all while using lovely dresses to communicate with the rebels myself." She brushed her knuckles under her chin in a coy gesture. "Aren't I clever?"

Marie raked in a sharp breath. *Utterly brilliant.* Alice's hand had gone limp, her eyes unblinking as she watched the two women converse across the table.

"I've heard all about you, Genevieve. Your dedication and loyalty, your conviction for our cause." Colette's gaze softened, considering Genevieve with something akin to kindness. Appreciation, perhaps. "You and your husband have asked to meet with me so many times over the last year. I'm sorry it had to be tonight, under these circumstances."

Genevieve grimaced, then asked in a quiet voice, "You are *ordering* me to do this?"

"No," Colette replied. "I'm pleading with you."

The woman blinked a few times, and her gaze slid to Marie and Alice. Her head tilted, eyes glazing over. She listened intently to something over her shoulder, and Marie's guts twisted violently.

"If they leave," Genevieve said a bit absently, "they have people who will pursue them. Dangerous people who will not let them disappear without causing trouble for all of us. That includes you, my Lady. Your involvement will be noticed, and may be revealed to the whole town."

Colette nodded, as if accepting the warning as premonition. "Then I will leave too. We'll leave behind some evidence that something horrible happened to us three. The town will think we are dead. That will keep my family, and the company, safe."

Genevieve looked pointedly at Marie. "And if *her* husband does not believe the evidence?"

That gave Colette pause. Her eyes shuttered. Marie wasn't

even given a chance to wonder if he would believe or not before her Lady said, "Don't worry about him. We will be poisoning Henri before we leave."

"*What?*" Marie expelled from a tightening chest.

Alice muttered under her breath, "Oh my stars."

Genevieve only rapped her fingers against the arm of her chair, tilting her head again as she said, "You're talking about murder."

Colette scoffed. "I'm *talking* about freedom and justice. Do not curl your lip at *me,* Genevieve. Our company has done far worse to those who have deserved it less. I ordered those deaths as well, and I do not recall you questioning my authority *before* you found out I was a woman."

Genevieve pursed her lips, her fingers stilling as she ruminated on that. Pity flooded her features as she turned once more to Marie and Alice.

A cold sweat broke out over Marie's body, accompanied by a wave of nausea so powerful, she ripped her hand away from Alice to press against the ache. The stress was going to make her sick. She swallowed the acid and kept her face as composed as possible, knowing that her luck was finally churning, changing.

It appeared a fortuitous turn.

Until Genevieve's head whipped to her opposite shoulder and her brow furrowed. "The tea," she muttered as her back went ram-rod straight. Her eyes snapped to Colette, narrowing in accusation. "*What did you put in the tea?*"

Marie vomited.

She pitched forward off the chair. Red, gritty matter gushed from her mouth, tasting of iron and rot. Porcelain shattered as her hands swept the table, as she attempted to catch herself on the edge, but her lungs burned, unable to fill back up with air as she heaved.

Her legs buckled, and her skull took the brunt of her collapse to the ground.

Shadows encroached on her vision, blinding her as her body convulsed against her will. She was only partially aware of the chaos above, of Alice's voice close beside her, crying, "What's happening to her? What have you given her—what have you done?"

Colette's response seemed to drift in from very far away, panicked. "I swear to you, I have no idea. It was only an herb. The peddler who sold it to me told me to steep it for courage."

Genevieve screamed, "*You fool.*"

"I—I don't *understand.* He drank it right in front of me. He told me it was miraculous, that it would drive away death and cowardice. I thought it would help us."

She roared back, "You have brought death upon us all."

Alice moaned in agony as the vomiting started up for her too.

Darkness swallowed Marie. The abyss took her and set fire to her veins. She dreamt of a stake, a rope around her waist. She dreamt she was burning alive. And there was nothing courageous in that place, nothing but tears and pain and anger. Anger that she had died now, after the suffering she'd been through, when she was so close to being free of it. She'd never felt such fury as this.

What felt like lifetimes later, a chill swept into the darkness, coating her in a layer of frost and moonlight. The ice seeped through her skin and sealed her into a glacial tomb.

All at once, the rope that held her slipped away, and Marie stopped dreaming.

When Marie woke, she did not stir her heavy limbs. Instead, she listened for the nothingness, the empty, the damnation, searching for an answer as to where she would spend eternity. She had not been optimistic in her mortal life… but in the end, she found perdition wasn't there to greet her.

She heard dripping and the low, muted rumble of what might have been a womb.

A whistling emerged from that rumble, the careless tune reverberating as if it were creeping around some corner of her mind. Light footsteps had her head arching, the floor against her cheek slick and glutinous. She inhaled a breath and groaned at the rawness of her throat. A throb resonated in her gums.

One of her eyes cracked open, and she stared into the void.

The floor glimmered with a thick sheet of blood. The drip came from the table towering over her. A mix of blood and amber water. *Drip, drip, drip.* She smelled the sulfur, the tainted bile, and sensed what felt like a thousand shadows bent to study her prone form.

Shards of porcelain lay scattered beneath her. Golden plant matter clung to the porous, broken edges, glittering like sunlight over moving water. It spoke to her without a voice.

We are the same now, you and I. Enduring, but not alive.

And that was when Marie realized her heart wasn't beating.

COLETTE

Colette was alone, surrounded by infinite darkness, and she couldn't move.

The shadows in front of her swirled with shades of grey, and the atmosphere was so heavy, it weighed on her, reflecting the oily stones of guilt in her gut. Her mind was fuzzy. It was as if she'd drunk several glasses of wine. She couldn't remember if that was true, but her tongue was thick and sour, so it was entirely possible. Possible that she'd indulged too much at a party and fell asleep, stark naked, in a room without windows.

At least, she assumed she was naked. She was shivering so hard.

Strands of glittering crimson and gold flickered to life, snaking around her, pulsing with light and fading in the next instant. And then darkness swallowed her again. A deeper emptiness, as if the light came only to show her how dark it really was. It came only to mock her.

She tried to recall her last waking moments.

A fresh chill coursed through her, and the haze finally parted. She remembered cradling Marie's head as she convulsed, watching the other women follow suit. The floor was flooded with red by the time the sickness took her too. *'You've brought death upon us all.'*

Was she dead? Were they all dead? If so, then it was her fault. And where was she now? An afterlife? It certainly wasn't heaven, but maybe it was hell—perhaps she would be tortured by this paralyzing, lonesome darkness for the rest of eternity.

The possibility scared her so much, she managed to curl her fingers in defiance. She bit her lip hard enough to taste iron. Inch by inch, she restored her body through pure strength of will.

She called weakly for Marie, but her own voice was the only one that echoed back.

Colette crawled through the darkness, crawled her way out of the emptiness. As she dug her nails into the ground and pulled herself forward, again and again, her surroundings began to shift. Those luminous strings returned, pulsing through her vision so brightly that she shut her eyes against them. A twinge of pain speared through her gums. Other sensations returned.

There was sticky liquid between her fingers, soaking her dress. A breeze. And then, she heard the screaming.

With a jolt, Colette snapped back to reality.

She lifted her head from the pool of ichor beneath her, blinking rapidly. Her physical body had never left the sitting room. She was still here. Head spinning, she looked around. The table and chairs were toppled, and those strings of red and gold were glowing in her periphery. She couldn't see past them well enough to make out the dark forms moving across the room. It had to be the other women. They were alive. But why were they screaming?

The ache hit her all at once.

Her abdomen cramped up, rumbling like thunder. A thousand needles pricked the skin along her spine, raising the flesh all over her body as a peculiar scent filled her nostrils. Warm and rich. Faintly sweet. Like a fresh pastry after weeks of stale bread.

Before she married her Lord, Colette endured plenty of weeks like that.

She was born to a dwindling fortune, bone-dry by the time she was a young woman, though her parents hid their poverty well. They had to. They raised their only daughter to save them, and she did. Even then, she knew the truth: love was a concept men used against beautiful women, to trap them in pernicious matches. Colette had never been susceptible to them, remaining as aloof and immoveable as the stars.

But this *scent*. It moved her. She couldn't deny it, and for a split second, she wondered if it might be the only thing she was capable of falling in love with.

The red threads coalesced across her vision, and she wasn't quite in control of her movements as she turned toward that delectable smell. She registered everything several moments after they happened. Far too late. The maid entered the sitting room through the kitchen, and as she took in the scene before her, terror twisted her face. The wide whites of her eyes gleamed as Colette launched at her. A strangled wail tore from her as Colette sank teeth into her throat.

There was not mercy, for such a concept was foreign to

Colette's new body. There was only sustenance and need and, in a small, strange way, desire.

Colette thought she woke up in hell, but she *knew* in that moment, as the maid's horror seared into her memory and moonlight illuminated the gnawed tissues she left behind, that this was the opposite. Hell had woken up in her. And there was nothing to remedy it, no heartbeat to remind her of what she'd been before. Before the blood.

She couldn't stop the thrill that raced down her spine.

And suddenly, there were arms around her neck. Her maid was holding her, pulling her closer, arching into Colette's embrace.

Eventually, the blood ran out, the way every precious, finite resource did. And though her belly sloshed with life as she sat back on her heels, Colette struggled to find her humanity in the aftermath. She stared down at the body, knowing she should feel badly for what she'd done, the death she caused. But it was a small, quiet thing—her guilt. The blood filling her veins and rushing through her ears was too loud to listen to it.

The *room* was too loud.

Crying echoed through the blood-soaked room, beckoning Colette's attention back to the dark figures she glimpsed before. As her thoughts and vision clarified, she saw them. Her gaze caught on Marie first, instantly, like flame to kindling. Her lovely blonde hair was brown from all the blood in it, her petite body shaking with silent sobs as she stood with her face tucked into Alice's shoulder. Colette suddenly realized that she was… *hiding*.

Reluctantly, Colette tore her gaze from Marie and looked at what she was hiding from.

The moment her eyes landed on Genevieve and what she held, she understood. She understood, and her heart seemed to cleave right in two, dropping into her stomach and churning her full belly.

A child.

His eyes stared up at the ceiling, dull and unseeing. There was no way to describe the sounds coming from Genevieve, except that it was a mother mourning, filled with enough self-hatred to burn her from the inside out. She clutched at the boy's chest, as if she might rip the heart out of it.

"Come back, return to me," she pleaded. "I will never hurt you again, I swear it."

Her cheeks were covered in red, the black ringlets clinging to them. It took a moment for Colette to realize it was coming from her eyes. She was crying blood.

Colette took an unsteady step toward them. "What happened?" she breathed.

Genevieve didn't acknowledge the whispered question, but then, Colette wasn't asking her.

Marie lifted her face from Alice's neck, pointedly staring in the opposite direction of the room, unable to look at the corpses behind her. Because yes, there were other bodies beside Genevieve—the butler and the groundskeeper and the only other maid assigned to this wing of the house. Judging from the state of Alice and Marie, they had their fill.

Marie stifled her sobs enough to say, "He came when we were first waking." Bloody tears coursed down her heart-shaped face, smeared in drying patches over her temples. It made Colette want to draw closer, touch her, comfort her. She wanted to lick her every tear away.

Colette didn't do that, though. She didn't move. She didn't

look at the boy in Genevieve's arms either. Like Marie, she couldn't face it. But Colette's reasoning had less to do with sensitivity, and everything to do with blame.

This was all her fault.

Alice was the only one looking at the wreckage. She stared at them all without a speck of emotion, her dark eyes hard and almost reverential. When Marie could not continue the explanation, Alice said flatly, "His father sent him. He walked in looking for Genevieve, and she was…overtaken."

All her fault.

Her fault.

Colette could barely see through her own tears, the dark drops gathering in her lashes. She took a slow step, and another, then quietly knelt in the muck beside Genevieve, keeping her eyes trained above the death in the grieving woman's arms.

If Genevieve noticed her proximity, she chose not to react.

The Lady waited, trembling, on her knees. She waited for Genevieve's cries and pleas to cease, waited for the tears to stop flowing and dry into crimson-black fissures down both cheeks. She waited for Genevieve to finally raise her head.

When those ice-blue eyes met her own, Colette held the gaze without flinching. She swallowed tightly and said, "I will never forgive myself for what has happened to him. I am…so sorry."

It felt inadequate coming out of her mouth. Inadequate and foolish. Whatever Genevieve decided she deserved for this, however she reacted to the apology, Colette would accept it.

But Genevieve only closed her eyes.

After a long moment, she bent and kissed her son's brow,

then tilted her head to listen to a shadow over her shoulder. In a crackly voice, she said, "We need to leave town while it is dark. We need a place to shelter ourselves from the sun. If we can't find one, we will need to bury ourselves in shallow graves along the road."

Marie exchanged a glance with Alice. They could not trust her, but there had never been more compelling evidence for Genevieve's all-knowing spirits than this: the four of them, alive but not really. Those spirits were real. They warned Genevieve away from the tea, and now they were warning them away from dawn. Their lives here were over. Colette knew that from the moment she'd followed Henri into the back room of the shop.

So they didn't ask questions. They didn't argue.

Genevieve wrapped her son in a sheet. At that point, Marie stepped away from Alice and walked to Colette's side, silently reaching out to take her hand. The three of them watched as Genevieve started a fire in the hearth and then methodically set the rest of the sitting room aflame.

Colette's throat tightened as the wallpaper began to curl, as smoke billowed toward the ceiling and the bodies of her staff caught the fire as well. She didn't even have time to whisper a farewell before Marie pulled her from the manor. And when the women emerged into the night, the town was quiet.

Too quiet, Colette thought, for what swirled in her veins.

The starry sky cast blue shadows along the main road, infinite darkness in one sense but a liberating gleam of hope in another. She was *free*. They all were. That excitement returned, tingling down into her fingertips. As they walked away from the manor and turned onto the main road leading out of town, Colette squeezed Marie's hand and gave her a tender smile. She didn't even care that Alice held onto her other.

Genevieve walked ahead of them, and it seemed like such a keen foretelling of what was to come. Drawn into the darkness by a woman who talked to it.

"Wait." Alice stopped short on the road. Her eyes were on Marie.

Alice tugged her closer, and Marie instantly let go of Colette's hand to be pulled in. Colette forced herself not to react. She only watched as Alice smoothed her hands over Marie's knotted hair and said, "There is one last thing we must do."

Marie's brow furrowed.

Alice stood a little straighter, smirking a bit as she added, "I think we can do better than poison now."

Colette's mouth flooded with a tangy substance, a film that tingled on her tongue and the seam of her lips. Her skin broke into gooseflesh as she realized what Alice was suggesting—the revenge Marie deserved.

Marie gazed back at Alice with wide eyes. She didn't object. And that made Colette incredibly proud of her, and of how far she'd come from the young woman she first met.

Colette stepped forward. "I'll come with you." If only to see it through.

Alice shot her a disparaging look. It was quickly assuaged by the smile blooming on Marie's face. She was brave enough right now, strong enough, to give him the end he deserved, but perhaps not brave enough to do it alone.

Genevieve spoke up from where she waited up ahead, her cloaking hanging heavy on her back and her face shadowed.

"I'll wait for you under the cover of the forest. Don't be long."

They nodded their agreement and diverged from the road, walking together over an uneven field, toward a shack in the distance. No. Colette was sure their particular brand of blood thirst would not spare them very long at all.

MARIE

Marie stared at the shabby front door, hesitating, her teeth aching as she ground them. Alice and Colette left her to enter the house alone. It was all part of *the plan*.

But she could hear him in there. Every minuscule movement. His heavy breathing and the low, senseless mumbles he made between urgent sips from some bottle. Usually, he'd be passed out cold by now; it was late, and the moon was high.

Instead, he was drinking himself mad and waiting up for her.

He wasn't going to get the chance to hurt her this time. Her body, however, remembered what it was like to be mortal and frightened. She couldn't stop trembling.

Slowly, she lifted her hand and grazed her fingertips over the flower wreath she'd threaded and hung on the door over the summer. It had been torn recently in one of Henri's drunken fits, when she managed to barricade herself alone in the bedroom and he'd gone through the rest of the house looking to destroy anything that he thought made her happy.

Little had he known that she made this wreath with Alice, one late afternoon in the shop together, and that was the reason she loved it so much. It still made her smile, even if it looked a little broken. He couldn't take that happiness from her. He couldn't touch her memories. The reminder gave her enough nerve to drop her hand to the doorknob and twist.

Marie rolled her shoulders back and pushed through the front door, the rusty hinges and floorboards creaking as she entered the house for the last time.

Their home was small. Only three rooms, and the largest encompassed the sitting area, the kitchen, and the small dining room. The moment she walked inside, she saw him sitting at the table. He held a mostly empty gin bottle, the liquid sloshing as he swung it back and forth above his lap.

Smirking, his eyes cut through the shadows of the entryway to find her. "Finally," he grumbled. "What took you so long, dear?"

The endearment spun webs of disgust in her belly. He always made love sound so scary, so hollow. This time, she didn't let herself fear him. She closed the door behind her and faced him, keeping her chin up as she took a step forward. The foul scent of urine filled her nostrils, and she paused. Glancing at the kitchen, her suspicions were confirmed.

He had been pissing in the corner of the kitchen again.

On another night, she might have immediately walked over to the puddle and began cleaning it, trying to appease his anger by getting on her knees. But what did it matter? She would be gone soon. They both would.

She took two slow steps, crossing the musty floor of the sitting area into the candle light spooling out from the dining table.

When Henri saw the state of her, he shot up straight in his chair, the bottle landing with a thunk on the rickety table. His gaze scoured her from head to toe. "What happened to your dress?" His lips curled in revulsion. "You look *awful*."

There was distress in his voice, but she wasn't fooled by it. Maybe he had planned on taking her body tonight, before the real punishment began, and the mess she'd showed up in staved off that desire. What a disappointment for him.

His gaze flicked up to her face. He considered her, the coolness of her expression, the utter lack of fear. "Ahh," he ran a palm over his beard. "I see."

Does he? Could he?

He smiled, displaying his grotesque, yellow teeth, chipped in places from picking one too many fights in the tavern. "She whipped you, didn't she? Broke your heart."

Marie didn't dignify that with a response, but her stomach turned, growling softly as her fury returned in full force.

Henri's unfocused eyes narrowed into slits as he laughed. "Oh, my dear, I wish I had been there to see that. I never understood what she saw in you, why she spoiled you and treated you like an equal when we both know you're no better than the dirt on her heels."

Marie's mouth tightened.

She'd once felt sorry for him, her husband. She knew too much about where he'd come from and what had been done to him, the reasons for his cruelty. He divulged too much when the liquor hit the wrong way. But she saw the truth now, saw it clearer than she ever had. Her every sense was sharpened to something like a razor's edge. And she knew the time for pitying him had ended a long time ago.

His sneer was a deep well of jealousy. He had always been

that way about *any* goodness she tried to claim for herself because he was so damn miserable on his own.

So, instead of reacting, she kept her mouth shut a little longer, gazing at him in that quiet but defiant way she'd learned to hold onto over the years, knowing it would infuriate him not to have access to her thoughts. Knowing that was always the one thing she *could* withhold from him.

"Thank the Light you brought the Lady to her senses tonight," he mused in her silence, his tone dripping with irritated amusement. "She won't even miss you."

Marie tilted her head, rubbing her fingers together at her sides. "You're right about one thing. I think the Light has finally decided to shine upon me, husband."

His clenched his jaw, the smile fading from his features. That hadn't been the response he expected. Nose flaring, his fist whitened around the neck of the gin bottle as he replied, "It's funny that you should speak about the Light so fondly when you are mere breaths away from being destroyed by it."

"I won't be destroyed by anyone."

He blinked. Leaning forward in his chair, he seethed, "How easily you forget about *me*, my dear."

Oh, she wished it was that easy. She was eager for the day when she could forget him entirely. Tonight was the beginning, the start of a new life without his poison in her ear and in her womb. Freedom was so close, she could taste it. Iron and dew and the cool, night air.

"Tell me, husband, how do you plan on doing anything to me?" Marie wondered aloud, letting her voice soften into a treacherous, liquid thing. "You can't even walk across the kitchen without toppling over, like some disoriented cow."

His head bobbed back as if she'd hit him. She was sure she would have felt better if she had.

Henri's eyes turned flinty as he rose from the chair. His cheeks bloomed with blood. Against Marie's best efforts, her teeth ached anew, venom welling under her tongue. He laughed, every inch of him edged in danger as he stalked toward her. "What did you say to me?"

At that moment, the window behind Henri slammed open. He jumped and twisted toward it, only to spin again when the front door echoed the bang. Marie felt a hand graze her waist. Then, nothing but the night breeze as it blew through the house.

By the time Henri's eyes landed on the now-gaping door, there was nothing to see. To him, the house was seemingly empty.

Sweat beaded on his forehead. "What was that?"

A thud resonated from the back of the house, just beyond the threshold on the other side of the kitchen. The bedroom. Henri's gaze followed the sound, and he looked in time to see the figure dip in and out of view through the darkness.

Henri staggered back a few steps, hitting the wall of the dining room as he exclaimed, *"Did you see that?"*

Marie raised an eyebrow and asked, "Did I see what?"

The knob in his throat bobbed. "A—a shadow," he replied quietly.

This might have been the first time Marie had ever seen him truly frightened. It fanned that fire in her gut. It made her lips curve up.

"Perhaps the gin is making you see things. It wouldn't be the first time."

He turned to her and hissed, "This is *real*."

"Then you *should* be afraid." She bared her teeth in a vicious grin.

"*You.*" He pointed at her with a trembling finger. "What kind of evil have you wrought on us?"

Her head tilted again to consider him, and she realized at once that she wasn't entirely in control of herself. Her body moved of its own volition. Overpowered by the natural instinct of a predator.

"I brought vengeful angels home to kill you, husband." She opened her hands on either side of her, welcoming his scrutiny. "And I am one of them."

His eyes flashed, and he shoved off the wall. "How dare you threaten me. You are *nothing*." He lumbered toward her, fast and large.

And for a moment, her body reacted before she could remind herself not to.

She reeled, flinching as he raised a calloused hand—and then he was gone. He was ripped backward in a blur of darkness. She heard a garbled scream.

Marie blinked in shock, and the world focused quickly enough for her to watch Alice tear out a chunk of Henri's neck with her teeth. He fell to his knees. Alice caught him before he collapsed entirely and spit the tissues out of her mouth.

Blood gushed, thick and dark over Henri's collar. She must have ripped into something vital. But she didn't let him bleed out.

No.

With a grimace, she slapped her hand over the wound and stopped up the surge of blood with her fingers. It wasn't going to save him. The blood still flowed, seeping between her digits. Henri's face was already paling as he clutched at her hand, adding pressure to his neck, the fear of death written all over his face. He must have known he wasn't bound for heaven, because his whispered prayers were frantic.

Marie just stood there, breathless, searching for a way forward.

"Colette," Alice called over her shoulder. "Take him."

The Lady emerged from the darkness, her face as impassible as Alice's. Without a word, she slipped into place behind Henri, and Alice stepped away.

Alice scowled at the sheen of blood on her hand. Stalking to the dining table, she swiped the gin and poured a portion of what remained over her palm, washing the stain away. Then, to Marie's surprise, she brought the bottle to her lips. Alice swished a mouthful of liquor and turned to spit Henri's own bloody gin all over his face.

He sputtered, "You monstrous whore."

Alice didn't react, didn't even look at him as she returned the bottle to the table.

Glaring through the liquor running down his face, Henri turned to Marie. He opened his mouth, as if to spout another insult her direction, but Colette's free hand shifted to his mouth, her fingers digging into his skin.

"One more word from you," she swore, "and I will break your jaw."

He wisely kept silent. His eyes remained on Marie's, searing into her like an accusation, like a promise. Marie could only hope there was no afterlife where he could haunt her. He would do it, if that was a possibility. He would dedicate his whole existence to making her suffer.

Marie's chest tightened. If she had a heartbeat, it would

have been pounding. Maybe this had been a mistake... to come back.

She didn't notice Alice had come to her side until she firmly grabbed the underside of Marie's jaw and guided her face toward her own. "Eyes on me, love."

The coaxing tone was enough to pull Marie out of her thoughts.

Alice's hazel eyes glittered with wickedness as she added, "I'm going to show him exactly what you thought of when he was on top of you."

Before Marie could realize what those words meant, Alice started hitching her dress. And then it sank in. What Alice wanted to do.

Marie's throat tightened, her mouth watering as she forced herself to catch Alice's arms. "Alice, we shouldn't—"

"Why not?" Alice grinned, her breath quickening as she continued to lift Marie's skirt. Marie, after all, wasn't fighting it with much force. "He can't do a thing about us anymore. It's just you and me."

Marie knew that wasn't true. They weren't the only ones in this room. She was stunned by her lover's brazenness, but her body was vibrating too—wrecked with desire. The change in her body had starved her in more ways than one, and she couldn't quite bring herself to care that they had an audience. Faintly, Marie knew it was more than just desire for Alice. Whatever predators had entered their bloodstreams, they were possessive creatures.

Alice finally slipped her hand under the hem of Marie's dress and found her slick heat.

Marie moaned softly. Her hands flew up to grip Alice's shoulders as those thin, dextrous fingers circled the peak between her thighs. She kept their gazes locked, even as her eyes fluttered. Even as Alice kissed her.

She tasted of gin and sin and… *his blood.*

The blood Marie dreamt of spilling herself so many times, when she only had her needle as an option. Now she had her teeth. Her hunger. The lingering traces of his blood were atrocious, rotten and sour, but she eagerly sipped it from her lover's tongue. The liquor swept into her mouth, burning away every awful memory she'd collected in this house and replacing it with love. Every roll of pleasure rolling down Marie's spine was more intense than she remembered.

It was revelation.

Marie moaned again, louder, giving herself over.

"That's right," Alice murmured, loud enough only for Marie to hear. "That's my beautiful girl."

Alice bit her lower lip in play. But the tingle that erupted under Marie's skin because of that nip was anything but playful. It was serious pleasure, merciless. A sticky-sweet resin trickled into her mouth, tasting acutely of Alice's soul. Slightly bitter, citrus and spice.

Marie was soaking Alice's hand. She heard the wet slide of those fingers against her sensitive tissues. And then she cried out as she speared to the peak of her pleasure.

"Listen to her," she heard Alice command. She was speaking over her shoulder. She was speaking to *Henri.* "These are the noises she makes for me, and me alone. All those times you hurt her just because you could, all the times you pretended she belonged to you—even then, her heart was mine."

Marie's eyes fluttered open, and she saw only Alice. Her hazel eyes, lit with satisfaction and anger and pride. Her mouth, parted in a faint smile. Alice didn't remove her touch. She kept stroking, urging Marie back to a place of fog and sunlight and rocky cliffs.

"You hear that, Marie?" Alice whispered. "You're *mine*."

That sent Marie soaring again, a pleasure so intense that her knees buckled. Alice held her upright. Then she withdrew her hand and cradled Marie's face. She kissed her once more, nodded—a soft, subtle encouragement.

Alice stepped aside.

Marie stared at the man kneeling before her. He was so still, she wondered if he was dead already. But as she drew closer, she saw the blood still flowing from his neck. She wasn't interested in drinking it.

They'd find another way to end him.

Colette returned Marie's stare with heavy-lidded eyes from where she crouched behind Henri. Her full lips were parted, but she barely seemed to be breathing as Marie approached the two of them. Marie tried to decode that look. Approval? Admiration? That was two things the Lady had never withheld from her.

But Colette's gaze weighed on her now, coating the room around them in a hazy, delicious hue of silver.

She couldn't help but wonder if *this* look meant something… *more*.

That was the reality, wasn't it? Now they were so much more than they were—stronger and fiercer. It was only natural that they might change in the way they acted towards one another. She hoped it would draw them closer together, especially Alice and Colette.

Marie took two more steps and paused when she saw the tears streaking down Henri's face. And yes, it was tears of frustration and rage, but *he* was the one crying this time. Marie smiled at him, and he started trembling.

He tried to speak, but the words were muffled under Colette's hand.

Colette snarled in warning.

But Marie only said, "I want to hear what he has to say."

Marie knew better than to expect words of regret or apology. He was too proud. Too horribly self-centered to admit he'd done anything wrong. So she wasn't surprised in the slightest when he spat, *"Disgraceful harlot."*

Colette looked at him like she was ready to follow through on her threat and shatter his jaw. Marie chuckled, and both Colette and Henri blinked in surprise.

"That may be true," she purred. "But at least I will rest easy knowing that no piece of me can ever belong to you again."

Unconcerned with where his soul would spend eternity, Marie made sure to give him a taste of her fury, her hell. The neighboring farms, of course, ignored the screams.

PART II

THE BLOOD

COLETTE

Decades passed in the red haze of immortality.

Colette saw no great difference in her way of living. She kept her love of fine materials and luxury and sweeping soirees, her love of grand rooms and brief affairs… but immortality was a proper shock for the rest of them.

Alice acclimated quickest. She understood the necessity for the parties that filled their nights, embracing them with the same sense of duty Colette was sure she embraced her mortal profession. She connected with the nobles of the city, infiltrating the best places alive at night to recruit guests from, and arranged deliveries of food and wine for the humans to feast on while *the beasts* fed on their veins. She was an excellent helper and proved so charming, Colette began to understand her appeal, if only just a little.

But Colette and Alice often had to *drag* Marie to these parties.

Over the years, Marie's timidness turned into something else. A sinister gleam that twinkled in her eyes every time she saw a man slurring his speech or leering at her figure. She preferred to prowl the darkest corners of the city for her meals, drinking twice as much as the rest of them, twice as often. Colette had a horrible suspicion that Marie actually held herself back… that the hunger she felt was deeper than the need the rest of them carried.

Colette wasn't brave enough to ask, but she sometimes wondered if her friend was unsatisfied with the life the four of them had settled into. If she longed for something *more.*

Tonight, at least, Marie had joined them eagerly in the ballroom of their estate.

The breeze drifting in through the open balcony was warm, tinted with the scent of fresh bread and citrus-infused honey. The sheer curtains billowed, glistening beneath the crescent moon.

Colette's entertainment for the night was a pair of males, strong and fresh and coarse enough to fascinate her. She couldn't remember their names, but they indulged her with wicked smiles and didn't care that she wanted them both at once… so she let them touch her as much as they dared. They dared quite a lot. But then, they were desperate for Colette to keep biting them.

She was straddling one of them—a noble from up the road.

His velvety tunic was parted, exposing his tawny brown neck and chest to her teeth. He moaned softly as she fed, squeezing her round hips in encouragement as she left her mark. She savored every drop. He tasted better than the other man had, like a summer rain and syrupy nectar. A ripe peach. Oh, it had been so long since she enjoyed a sweet peach tart. And he was as good as the real thing.

His wounds wept rivulets of red down his abdomen, and she took her time licking each one before lifting her head.

The noble smiled at her, his dark brown eyes drooping from the effects of her venom. His hands slid up to appreciate her curves. "How exquisite you are, my darling."

Wrinkling her nose, Colette twisted in his lap and surveyed the rest of the room. She hated when men tried to trap her with affectionate words. She'd heard all of it by now, a thousand times over. Darling was her least favorite, considering that was what her late husband used to call her. Even now, she could hear his voice in her head echoing it. *'Darling Colette, my life, my Light.'* He couldn't have been more deluded.

He died a few weeks after she left, but that didn't surprise her; she'd expected him to die many years before that. Since then, their sons had grown up brilliantly and had sons of their own. Grandsons. The last time she'd checked on them, they seemed fine. Happy, even.

They were all happier for her leaving.

Colette's eyes skipped across the room. So much vibrant color in the satin and silk, the draperies and furniture. Rusty orange and forest green. Accents of blue opal. Bare skin. Blood swirling, dripping, glimmering against the ivory marble floor.

Then her gaze caught on a curtain of golden hair, and everything else paled in comparison.

Marie fed on a male in the maroon chaise across the room. She knelt on the cushion, her face buried in his neck. A steady trickle of blood coursed down the male's pale chest, staining the sleeve of Marie's sapphire-blue nightgown as she held him in place. But he arched into her mouth like a heart reaching for heaven. His eyes fluttered sleepily as his head rocked against the back of the chaise, thoroughly enthralled.

They prepared their guests before allowing them into the manor. Everyone was told exactly what to expect, and they were then carefully taught to enjoy it. Not that it was difficult to convince them.

One of the first things the women discovered about their new bodies was the power they held in their teeth. In the venom they produced. One bite, and their prey was effectively immobilized, overwhelmed by the waves of pleasure their venom stirred. No alcohol, no herb in all the earth, could compare.

Marie decided she'd finally had enough and pulled off of the male, even as he whimpered in protest and tried to grab at her loose curls. Dodging his fingers, she gripped the male's shoulder and tipped him forward, sending him sprawling on the marble floor at her feet. Then she smiled wickedly and crawled across the cushion.

Colette's skin tingled.

She wondered, for what felt like the hundredth time in as many days, what it might be like to be on the receiving end of *that* smile. She wondered what it might be like… to be Alice.

Alice, who had been sitting on the male's other side, sipping from his wrist, laughed and licked the remnant blood off her lips before falling forward to capture Marie in a kiss.

Colette forced herself to look away.

She told herself not to watch, knowing it would only make the twirl in her stomach that much worse. There was an actual *sickness* attached to the sight of them touching. Mostly because they did it so frequently, so openly, now. Colette couldn't help but feel affronted by it, by *them*, like love was only shown to her in some spite-fueled game run by the universe.

How long would she last without love, be happy without it? That was the question.

There was so little else for her to want once she was no longer human. Once time opened up and the urgency for wealth and success evaporated. Once she discovered that blood ruled everything *but* her dead heart.

So she kept chasing love, kept trying. Truly, she did.

Colette turned to the male beside her, the one who was caressing her thigh with a stupid drunk grin on his face. His blond hair was mussed from where her fingers had tangled in it a few minutes ago. The bite she made on his chest was still weeping. His glazed eyes flicked excitedly between her and the noble.

They'd come together, and she had seen them strolling through the city at night many times before, arm-in-arm, a noble and his second. Maybe more. Perhaps that was why they were so good at sharing.

The blond's fingers ventured higher, slipping between the panels of her white nightgown. His entire body jolted when he touched the dagger strapped there. He blinked in confusion, his brow furrowing as he pushed away the sheer material to look at it. She still carried it with her, even after all these years. She knew she didn't need it now like she did when she was mortal, but its weight comforted her in ways her new body couldn't.

It was the only reminder she had of the humanity, the frailness, that she'd lost.

Colette continued twisting on the noble's lap, fully facing the blond and removing his fingers from the hilt of her dagger.

She smiled and let her legs fall open. An offering. Only a single panel of white chiffon veiled her sex, and the male quickly forgot his fascination with the weapon as she tugged him off the chaise and onto his knees before her.

The noble leaned forward and trailed gentle kisses up the back of her neck, his hands slipping around to untie her nightgown as his blond partner slid the panels apart between her thighs.

She sighed as the blond's mouth found her core, her neck arcing as the noble nibbled on her ear and his hands found her bare breasts. They worked in tandem to consume her in pleasure.

Waves of heat rolled up her spine as their teeth and tongues scraped her skin, as their soft fingers massaged her curves and readjusted her position, inch by inch. She knew better than to close her eyes. Knew what terrible desires and fantasies lived in the darkness of her mind. So she watched them work her body into a flame, watched the blond head move between her legs. Their brown and ivory skin swirled together as her eyes fluttered, as she tried to focus.

But looking at Marie was like scratching a bug bite settled under Colette's skin. She couldn't stop itching at her curiosity, at the madness of Marie's beauty, both inside and out.

Colette could remind herself to look away a thousand times or more, but she always came back, and hated herself more for it in the end. Because wherever Marie was, Alice was. And so Colette was forced to acknowledge her envy, too. Her emptiness.

But that wasn't enough to stop her.

Her eyes slid up and found the women on the other side of the room. Fresh blood dripped from Marie's smile. She impatiently grappled with Alice's violet gown, attempting to tug her closer. But Alice was laughing, her eyes bordering on delirious as she shifted further and further away, teasing Marie into a frantic state of need. Alice's neck was bleeding. Marie had fed on her, filled her with venom.

The first time Colette saw them bite each other like that, she wasn't sure what to think.

It quickly became clear that their venom had the same effect on them as it did the humans. Only, with them, there was no risk of drinking too much. There was no coercion. For Alice and Marie, drinking from each other was a loving ritual. A possessive act. Yet another thing Colette secretly wished to experience, but knew she never would.

She contented herself watching them dance. Heat swelled between her thighs, and maybe it was because of the tongue stroking it, the coaxing hands all over her, but she heard a whisper of truth she tried her best to ignore.

Seeing Marie prowl forward on her hands and knees, her gown disheveled and blood painting her mouth, affected Colette. She looked celestial. Slaughter incarnate.

Alice's back hit the curved end of the chaise. She ran out of room to continue the chase. Marie took Alice's face in her hands and kissed her deeply, scooting closer until she had Alice pinned in. Alice dragged her hands up Marie's figure, returning the kiss until she had her hands wrapped firmly around Marie's neck. She used that leverage to push her away, to nip at Marie's lip. Alice gave her a dark, challenging smile.

And Marie snapped.

She broke Alice's hold on her throat and grabbed her around the waist, twisting them both so that she could straddle Alice's thighs. Alice laughed, but that was quickly muffled by a forceful kiss. Marie moved with a sense of urgency. Her hands flew to the hem of Alice's gown and pushed it up, exposing Alice's sex. Marie knelt up and inched forward on her knees without breaking the kiss. And a sense of urgency pervaded Alice's movements as well. She hitched Marie's nightgown, her freckled, pink skin gleaming in the candlelight. Colette's gaze caught on the curve of her hips, the veiled shadow between her thighs as she aligned herself with Alice.

Their bodies became a tangle of legs as they rearranged their limbs and started grinding.

Colette lifted her bottom off the noble's lap and reached between them. His trousers were already unlaced, and it took almost no effort to free him. Once he caught on to what she wanted, he quickly helped notch himself at her entrance and pushed in.

She reached down and threaded her fingers into the blond male's hair, encouraging his mouth back to her sex. To her delight, he acquiesced with a smile, his long fingers digging into her hips.

Colette lowered herself the rest of the way and rode them with abandon.

The noble slid his hands down her front, gripped her inner thighs and spread her wider, then held her in place as he rutted up into her. Her fingers tightened in the golden hair between her legs, and she tried her best not to imagine someone else's face beneath it. The blond groaned, and one of his hands dropped into his lap.

She gave her body over to them, letting the sensations of their joining roll through her. She savored every raw scent, every moan, every pinch and stroke and thrust.

But her eyes… her eyes remained on the beautiful blonde woman moaning across from her.

Colette had never watched them like this, in the midst of pleasure. A small voice in her head told her it was inappropriate, even if they were indulging each other in the center of the party. This wasn't the first time they made love in the open. She'd seen glimpses before, but this was the first time Colette had been tempted to see it through to the end.

Alice had opened the front of Marie's gown and was fondling her breasts, her fingers circling Marie's pert nipples.

Marie's eyes closed. She whimpered—short, sharp gasps as they all continued to move.

As if sensing Colette's eyes, Alice glanced up at her from her prone position on the chaise. She blinked in surprise and then her eyes narrowed, but Colette didn't flinch. There wasn't a speck of attention for Colette to spare her. All of it belonged to Marie.

Alice snarled and sank her teeth into the soft skin of Marie's breast.

Colette couldn't breathe. She reached back and looped a hand around the nape of the noble's neck and took possession of the rhythm, urging him faster. He obliged, and she started panting. Marie was rising to the peak of her pleasure too. Colette could tell. Marie's lips parted in the perfect little oval.

Colette's vision blurred around the edges.

Marie threw her head back in ecstasy. Their gazes locked, and Colette tumbled into a gray-blue sea. For the first time, Colette heard a tone, a note, a mere *vibration* of the music that Marie and Alice must hear every second of every day. She felt it radiate down into her bone marrow.

Release ricocheted through her like a crashing cymbal.

She screamed, only vaguely aware of the echoing cries to either side of her. But the descent from that peak was swift and staggering. Her eyes fluttered. The world was so unreasonably dark in comparison to the stars she'd just seen. It was all too clear in that moment.

Marie and Alice lazily kissed each other in the distance, their bodies wholly intertwined. If Marie had realized what passed between them a moment before, she'd already forgotten. It didn't mean anything to her.

Colette shouldn't have watched.

Kisses were being brushed across her shoulder, along her inner thigh. But Colette refused to acknowledge them. She refused to acknowledge any of the punishing thoughts running through her mind. She untangled herself from the men's worshiping hands and retreated to a corner of the room where no stray eye would see the tears she shed.

ALICE

If Marie wiggled her fantastic rear end against Alice even one more time, she was going to combust.

They danced lazily to the strings and bells bouncing through the room. Marie moved like a goddess, even as euphoric and mentally distant as she was.

Alice usually wasn't one for dancing, but when Marie was in this wonderful of a mood, there was no denying her. This creature. This insatiable being, drunk on blood and sex, was easier to watch than the dark one who otherwise walked the streets at night. Marie did not smile then. She did not dance. And those nights certainly did not end with Alice's tongue between her legs.

Loving Marie was like riding bareback on a wild stallion, the wind whipping at every angle and the threat of death looming underfoot. At once exciting and terrifying. Death became a game of how tightly she could hold on. How long.

Except, in reality, she knew she couldn't die. Not by horse or arrow, nor any other man-made brutality. There was very little that could truly hurt her. She'd lost track of how many things she tried.

Not because she wanted to die. But because sometimes she worried about the day when she might want to.

Her body was unbreakable, and her soul was anchored firmly in this body. Skin mended. Organs healed. Her spirit, on the other hand… that was something that could be destroyed. All it would take is one loss. If she lost the woman in her arms, if she lost Marie, she would have no desire to continue on in immortality. So she tested their limits to know how to protect them both from the worst, from the permanent.

There were two things that proved significantly harmful. Fire and sunlight.

A little bit of either couldn't kill, but they did maim. Luckily, Genevieve and her horrid spirits had already warned against them, so when Alice was tempted to explore the elements for herself, she only stretched a hand beyond the curtains into the morning sun. It hadn't ended well. She'd wrenched back from the window with a burnt hand, her skin ignited with flame and smoke and reduced to a pile of ash within seconds. The recovery was slower than anything her immortal body had experienced up to that point, and it took several feedings to restore what she lost.

She still felt a twinge in her right hand every night just before dawn, as if her body were recalling the sun's kiss, and its betrayal. A scorned lover to each of them.

Speaking of which…

Alice's eyes slid to the right, past Marie's writhing body to the far wall of the ballroom. A curvy figure sat in the windowsill, staring up at the moon, the night beyond shrouding every detail except for her hair, those copper strands gleaming slightly beneath a nearby candelabra.

She did *not* like the way Colette watched Marie while she was climaxing.

Colette shouldn't have been looking at them at all, but feeding in the same room made them cross all sorts of boundaries without meaning to. An accidental brush of bodies. Lingering glances. All natural, and unavoidable. This time, however, it had felt intentional.

A low growl rumbled through Alice's chest, and her hands slid roughly up Marie's sides.

Marie shivered and spun to face Alice, looping her arms around Alice's neck as she smiled up into her brooding expression. "Hungry again?"

Her smile soothed the sharp envy rising in Alice. Not enough to return the smile, or to gentle her fingers before wrapping them possessively around Marie's throat, but just the *tiniest* amount. A drop in her ocean of worry.

"I'm always hungry for you." Alice's voice was less than a rasp.

Marie kept smiling, her eyelids drooping as she tilted her chin up and to the side, baring her neck in an offering. Alice's mouth flooded. It was the worst kind of temptation. To lose herself in Marie's blood all over again. To sink her teeth into that lovely skin and catapult them both to heaven for a while longer.

But Alice's mind raced as she lowered her mouth to Marie's neck, her thoughts spiraling into endless darkness as she dragged her nose down that ivory column of velvet.

"My love?"

"Mmm?" Marie was arching now, her chest thrusting into

Alice's. But Alice kept her teeth to herself. She had a question to ask, and she needed an uninhibited answer.

Alice pressed a kiss to the space under Marie's ear and whispered, "Have you ever considered taking someone else to your bed?"

Marie stiffened. Slowly, she leaned back, looking up at Alice with something like hurt in her eyes. Alice tracked every blink, waiting for any hint of proof that it was true. Alice told herself that it didn't matter if it was. She didn't wish for Marie to want for anything, and it was clearer now more than ever that she was struggling. No amount of blood could satisfy her, and maybe… maybe it was the same for her heart.

But Marie only shook her head and said, "Of course not."

She seemed to mean it.

Alice squeezed her waist. She forced a teasing tone as she said, "I can't be the only person you've ever found attractive. There are beautiful women who come in and out of this room every night."

"I don't understand why you're asking this," Marie mumbled, stepping back. "I love you."

"Eternity is a long time to be shackled to me, Marie."

Alice was surprised Marie had lasted *this* long.

Marie's eyes widened, and her head bobbed back. "Do *you* desire someone else?"

Alice's entire body went cold. She hadn't said the right thing; she'd given Marie the wrong idea. Could she do anything right? Blood stung the back of her eyes, but she quickly blinked them away before Marie could see. Mentally berating herself, she wrapped her arms around Marie's shoulders and drew her closer, even as she resisted. Even as the hurt coiled tighter in her eyes.

"No," Alice swore, her voice leaving no room for doubt.

The muscles in Marie's back instantly loosened. Her brows furrowed instead, her fingers anxiously rubbing at the front of Alice's gown. "Then what have I done to make you think I would want anyone else?"

The words caught in Alice's throat.

Because… everyone left eventually. Her father, her siblings, even the distant aunt she ran to when her mother died and she had no one else. She wished it was always as simple as separation by death. But the truth was that most of them just couldn't stand to be around her—she could tell—even when she tried her best not to be an imposition. No one understood her, her child-like quirks that embarrassed those around her and her mind that just never stopped spinning. She thought too much, and it spilled over her lips too often. That was what they said about her, to her face and behind her back. *Too much, too much, too much.*

Every once in a while, when the world grew too quiet and her mind too loud, Alice wondered if she was the one who made her mother sick. Had she shared too much of herself, wore on her mother's nerves until there was nothing left to keep her healthy? Had her mother been too weak to bear it?

More than likely.

It was obvious why everyone left Alice after that. They ran before she could drive them to death as well. She didn't blame them.

Alice kissed Marie. A gentle, appreciative kiss. "You've done nothing. Please, don't misunderstand me. I've had more than my share of men and women alike when it was my job to do so, but I'm the only one you've ever chosen to be intimate with. I just want you to be happy. And if that means giving you space and permission to explore—"

"If I explore," Marie interrupted, her fingers tugging sharply on the front of Alice's gown. "I only want to do it with you at my side. I don't want any space." Her eyes burned with honesty.

Alice smiled, reveling in the hundreds of moths fluttering in her stomach, crowding the flame that Marie had sparked there. That settled it. Whatever there was between Marie and Colette, it could never go anywhere. If Alice didn't want to go there with Colette, then neither did Marie. And one thing was for certain:

She was never going to crawl into bed with that crafty, miserable, admittedly devastating, woman.

COLETTE

Colette was two bottles deep in self-loathing when she felt a tap on her shoulder.

She looked up from where she sat on the windowsill and found herself towered over by a lean, black suit. The woman in it was smiling at her. It was a shy sort of grin, the sort that made her mauve lips thin and stretch until a sliver of white teeth gleamed through the dark. Her skin was the loveliest shade of reddish-brown, like that of a fine, wet clay.

The woman's suit was silken, obviously expensive and perfectly tailored. It took every speck of Colette's remaining sense to keep from reaching out to touch the fabric. Her braided black hair blended seamlessly where it fell over each shoulder.

Colette set the wine bottle down and twisted to face the stranger more fully, letting her bare feet hover just above the marble floor.

It was rare for Colette to come across a feminine who wore pants, or the reverse. But every once in a while, they would come through the ballroom, as curious about this manor as the rest of the city. All were welcome.

"You weep blood," the woman said.

Colette's hands flew to her cheeks, feeling the dried streaks there. It was an odd, almost *rude* thing for the stranger to point out, without so much as an introduction to precede it. Colette might have indeed been offended, if it wasn't for the woman's expression.

The stranger stared at her with alarming curiosity, her luminous brown eyes flicking up and down Colette's body. When Colette didn't immediately respond, she leaned in... as if she couldn't quite help herself. One of her petite shoulders braced the wall beside the windowsill, and her fingers rubbed together in front of her stomach. There were stains on her fingertips. Black dust. *Charcoal.*

She was an artist. And a successful one, judging from look of her.

Colette rubbed at her flaky cheeks. "Are you mentioning it because you're concerned, or do you simply wish to die?"

"Your tears are a difficult thing to capture without red pigment."

It wasn't an answer, but Colette didn't get the chance to demand one. The woman immediately plucked a kerchief from the breast pocket of her suit and wetted it with her tongue. Then she stepped closer and lowered the material to Colette's face.

Colette's head swirled with too much wine to react as the kerchief moved against her cheek, erasing her tears.

The full weight of the gesture registered and Colette thought about pulling away, but the kerchief had already moved on to her other cheek. The woman smiled again. Her brown skin creased delicately at the corners of her eyes and Colette was suddenly tempted to touch her there too.

Then Colette remembered that she'd said something about paint.

"You've attempted to paint me?" she asked.

The stranger took a small step back and folded the kerchief between her fingers before tucking it away. Her lips tightened. "No, not paint. Just sketches, with the supplies I can easily carry in and out of here."

She hesitated a moment, then she pulled a leather-bound booklet out of her coat that was about the size of her palm. Opening the booklet, she tilted the pages toward Colette. The parchment was filled with lines and patches of smudged charcoal. Colette couldn't quite decipher the image from this angle, but she could tell it was impressive for a sketch.

"It's amazing to me," the woman mused, pulling a nub of charcoal from her pocket and adding a few lines to the page. Her eyes flicked from Colette's face and back down, "how much I forget once I leave this room. Every detail blurs. I sit down at my easel when I get home, and I just stare at it for hours."

She rolled her shoulders and snapped the booklet shut, her eyes locking with Colette's as she tilted her head to one side. "Can you tell me why that is?"

It was part of the preparation for every mortal who came to their manor. As long as they were in this room, their visitors knew everything they needed to. They knew about the feedings. The orgies. The women's terrifying, true natures. But the moment they left, they would forget everything that happened. They would go home, to their families, to their normal lives, and if anyone asked, they would simply say that the manor hosted the finest parties in the city.

It was another sliver of the impossible, of *magic*—the women's ability to scramble human minds with nothing but their gaze and a few careful words.

But Colette shrugged and slumped against the wall of the windowsill. "That sounds like a question for your muse."

"You *are* my muse."

Colette blinked in surprise. The woman had said it with such certainty. "What do you mean?"

The stranger put away her sketch book and braced her palm on the wall above Colette's head, her other hand landing on the small of her waist. She was rather shapely. Tall. Colette wondered what her figure might look like without all those layers.

Those wandering thoughts were interrupted when the woman said, "I hardly know myself. For months, I've been coming here. And for months, I leave with a full sketchbook and absolutely no memory of drawing the pictures inside of it. I leave with sketches of *you*. What is this place? What are you?"

The woman had guessed it then, that they were not human. It was unusual for a guest to look beyond the ecstasy, beyond the room. In all the years they'd lived in this city, she was the first to ask questions. Who was this woman who dared risk her life for the truth? Why wasn't she scared?

"I'm a lady," Colette replied.

"You are *more*."

Colette slid off of the windowsill and stood. The woman didn't shift, didn't drop her arm or push away from the wall.

They were close enough to share air. Colette studied her. Those narrowed eyes. The baby hairs curling around her face.

Colette reached up and twisted one of those frizzy curls around one finger.

"Are you a ghost?" the woman whispered, her eyes softening. "Am I haunted by you?"

Colette dropped her hand to the suit, admiring its material without restraint, without shame. Her fingertips lingered against the lapel as she lifted her chin and asked, "What is your name?"

"Giselle." It was little more than an exhale.

Colette could almost taste her. Like freshly bloomed irises, slightly sweet and extraordinarily fragranced. She held back the excitement bubbling in her chest. "Can you keep a secret, Giselle?"

Giselle licked her lips and said, "Something tells me I wouldn't be able to betray you even if I wanted to, even if I were to try."

How right she was.

"My dear," Colette murmured, her tone a bit absent. She ran a hand up her shoulder, fingering the thick braid there. "You've entered a house of beasts. Murderesses."

"Hmm. Is that all?"

Colette lifted a brow, the effervescence in her chest turning to amusement. "Isn't that enough?"

"Not really," Giselle admitted with a breathless laugh, ducking her head to look at the lack of space between them. "The better question is whether you have a desire to kill *me*, or any of the other people in this room."

Colette wasn't sure where this conversation was leading,

but it intrigued her more and more the longer it went on. She shook her head. "I don't have that desire."

Giselle looked up into Colette's eyes and smiled. Such a breathtaking smile. "I guessed as much. Any woman with wealth and independence like this would have needed to kill for it. A husband or a father. I don't judge you for it either way. There are many in this country who wish they had the nerve to do the same."

Just like that, all the pieces of this mysterious woman fell neatly into place.

"When did you become a widow?" Colette asked.

Giselle's smile faltered, then shifted like a breeze changing directions. Her lips curved with secretive pleasure. "I was sixteen. So several years ago, now."

"My condolences," Colette said, though she didn't sound very consoling at all. Not that it mattered. Giselle wasn't sad, or sorry.

"What about you?"

Colette shrugged. "It's been a long time."

Giselle looked at Colette like an artist considering her work: with slicing judgment and a glimmer of pride. She said, "I know you're not going to tell me what you've done to me, but perhaps you will allow me to bring my canvas and paints next time. So I can capture you properly."

Colette counted Giselle's rapid heartbeats, letting them ground her. *Tha-thump. Tha-thump.* "Perhaps."

"And let me remember you?" Giselle ventured, stepping closer.

A tempting request, albeit dangerous. An artist painting a monster, remembering what should be forgotten, what they'd all worked so hard to keep in the shadows. But... well,

Colette was curious what that canvas might look like. The scent of Giselle hit her again. A wave of iris and iron that made her mouth water, made her lean in.

She didn't often feed on women. It was an intimacy, to sink your teeth into someone's flesh and sip from their veins.

Colette discovered that it was easier to exercise control over her hunger when other senses were involved, when she was touching her victims in more ways than one. That was why they started hosting the parties. Instead of being overwhelmed by the blood and accidentally killing someone, she could distract herself with sex. It kept her present enough to spare them. And since she'd learned that trick, she fed exclusively on willing, handsome men. There was no shortage of them.

Tonight, however, it felt as though Giselle was beckoning her towards a dark tunnel. A passage. She couldn't see the end of it, but she knew there was something waiting for her on the other side.

Her stomach stirred with an oily ache. Without meaning to, her gaze slid beyond Giselle to scour the rest of the room and instantly landed on the two women dancing in front of the manor's harpist. Marie and Alice spun slowly, intoxicated, lost to the music. Lost in love. And Colette abruptly wondered if she'd been doing this wrong all along, if she'd been *trying* with all the wrong people.

Maybe the person she needed looked less like the men she'd sought out, and more like...

Colette looked at Giselle. Her smile had softened into a sweet, patient thing, and Colette couldn't stop from leaning in even further, until there was no space left between them. The suit coat was soft, giving beneath Colette's fingers as she clutched the fabric. She held Giselle in place. Held her fast and firm. She'd made her decision, then. She was going to do this.

She brought her mouth to Giselle's ear and whispered, "If you taste as wonderful as you smell, I might consider it."

Giselle's breath caught, her body stiffening slightly as Colette's lips grazed her neck.

Her gums throbbed in anticipation. She'd just fed, and already it was back—the unending hunger. Sometimes her hunger burrowed so deep, she became convinced she thirsted for something more than human blood. Most nights, she forced herself to feel content with half-satisfied. And that was so incredibly reflective of her entire life, entire existence up to this point. Especially the time she spent as a mortal.

She took everything she desired back then and still felt incomplete. It should have been enough. Her family and their home and the freedoms she'd been given. More than most women received in that time, nobles included. She'd had enough. She told herself that so many times, it eventually rang like the truth in her ears.

Immortality exposed those lies, and there was no deluding herself about them a second time. A piece of herself was missing. And that piece had nothing to do with the hunger.

She siphoned all of that confusion, all of that hunger and need into this embrace. Her arms snaked around Giselle's waist and tugged her flush against her front.

Colette pressed a kiss to Giselle's collar, and her body swayed forward. Colette lifted her hands to the top of Giselle's blouse, focusing on the buttons there, but Giselle caught her wrists. That was enough to bring Colette out of her all-consuming desire. She pulled back an inch and met Giselle's panicked gaze.

"Why?" she breathed.

Colette's brows lowered over her eyes. "Why what?"

"Why do you drink our blood?"

Colette felt her lips purse. She wasn't sure how honest to be, how honest she *could* be since she barely had any semblance of truth for herself. "Because," she said carefully, "all life has a cost, and this is mine." The fear. The guilt. The blood.

Giselle's hands loosened on Colette's wrists, but she couldn't determine whether it was in surrender or in consideration.

Colette added quickly, "What I take from you, you won't miss. I promise to make you love it." Colette tugged lightly on the end of Giselle's braid, smirking.

Giselle nodded. A trace of unease lingered in her eyes, but she removed her hands from Colette's wrists and dropped them to her supple hips. Colette took it as permission to draw closer, slowly, giving ample time for Giselle to stop her if she wished to. Giselle didn't stop her. In fact, she swayed forward as well and wrapped her arms around Colette's neck before covering Colette's mouth with her own.

It was a shock. Kissing a woman.

Giselle's lips were warm and plush, the antithesis of every seduction Colette had made over the last few decades. The taste of her was a garden, bursting with vibrant shapes and colors and scents. Lavender honey. Sun-steeped tea.

Was this what she'd been missing? This effortless beauty, this… softness? It was enough to make a grown woman, even a *beastly* one, weak in the knees.

Colette felt as though the floor had fallen out from under her as her stomach plummeted. As her head spun. But no. The two of them had simply thrown themselves so far into the kiss that they lost their balance and collided with the wall.

Giselle gasped as her back took the brunt of the fall, and Colette took that opportunity to deepen the kiss. She slid her tongue between Giselle's parted lips, exploring the woman's mouth with eager, conquering strokes. Pressing into Giselle, Colette reveled in the alignment of their bodies. The symmetry. Soft to soft; curve to curve.

Sparks lit under Colette's skin, rolling in waves across her chest, hardening her nipples, and searing her down to the tips of her fingers. The fingers now hastily unbuttoning Giselle's blouse.

Colette was feeling so much, her thirst becoming so acute, that she sensed the rhythm of Giselle's pulse. It echoed through her core. *Tha-thump. Tha-thump.* Life and luminous arousal. Her inner thighs grew damp as she finally exposed Giselle's neck to the air. Their hips moved together, causing glorious friction. And in the back of her mind, Colette wondered if Marie could see them… if Marie would even notice if they coupled right here in the corner.

There was only one way to find out.

But as Colette brushed her canines down the length of Giselle's throat, worshiping the preferred vein, the woman jerked back. "Wait."

Colette might have voiced her displeasure if Giselle didn't look so frightened. Her eyes were wide, glassy. Though her cheeks were flushed and her lips had swelled, there was a hardness to her appearance, as if all her muscles in her back and shoulders were tensed.

"Just tell me first," she pleaded, "so I may prepare myself. How much is it going to hurt?"

Colette leaned back, but only far enough for the fear in Giselle's eyes to abate. "Silly woman, why do you worry about this?" she demanded. "You've watched me feed before. You must have seen how pleasurable it is for those I choose to embrace."

Giselle slowly shook her head. "I never watched them," she whispered. "I only watched you."

Colette forgot to breathe for a moment. She'd been desired for as long as she could remember. But this felt... different. Maybe it was because Giselle was an artist, but she made Colette feel truly seen—like she looked past the fangs and immortal vanity to the ripped shreds of humanity beneath them.

"I'll show you first. Come."

Colette took Giselle's hand and led her to the chaise she'd fed on earlier. There was a man there now, lounging lengthwise across the cushions with nothing but a blanket draped across his hips. He shared a cluster of grapes with a woman who sat on the floor beside him.

When Colette reached the chaise, she let go of Giselle's hand and shooed the other woman away. The man on the chaise noticed her focus on him and sat up. Colette vaguely recognized him, and he presented his bare thigh to her in a way that suggested he'd been fed from plenty of times. Colette didn't waste time on greetings. Her body was thrumming with desire, her skin burning with the weight of Giselle's eyes. The sooner she showed her there was nothing to fear, the sooner she could explore this new facet of need she'd discovered within herself. She spared only one glance across the room, unable to stop herself.

But Marie wasn't looking.

Colette wasn't sure why she tortured herself this way, over and over, while knowing the truth in her heart. Marie would never look her direction.

Colette turned her attention to the pulsing artery under her fingertips, the warmth of this flesh. This was all she needed. Blood and sex. And perhaps companionship with someone. She wanted that so badly, she was willing to do anything to get it. Love might not be possible, but true companionship was a possibility so real, she could practically taste it.

The blood called to her once again, so she lowered her head to that rushing vein, submitting to her beast for another moment, another night, casting her worries into the familiar river of crimson.

It was then that the doors to the banquet hall burst open, and all the air stole out.

Genevieve sauntered in, the edges of her cloak rippling as she crossed the room and aimed for the chaise where Colette sat.

Behind her, she tugged along a dirty, curly-haired little boy.

COLETTE

"What have you done?" Colette rasped, slowly rising from her seat.

Her limbs began trembling, but she ignored them and stalked forward. In her peripherals, she noticed the way the room seemed to stutter. Their guests turned as one to observe the child.

Children were *not* permitted here, ever. For obvious reasons.

Colette's eyes locked briefly with the young boy's. He'd been crying, but wasn't now. His face was stained with so many tracks, Colette knew he'd simply run out of tears.

That was when Colette realized she had blood dripping down her arm. She'd been so distracted, she didn't notice that the artery she just fed from spurted and covered her fingers.

She quickly licked it away.

Genevieve smiled as they met in the center of the room, a mad gleam in her eyes. Colette saw the dried blood on

Genevieve's hand. The one she used to drag the boy along behind her. It was as if he'd scratched at her hard enough to break the skin over and over. There was no evidence of wounds other than the blood. Their bodies healed too quickly for scars.

Mud caked the boy's clothes, and blood was streaked through his hair. Not his own blood, from the scent of it. Usually, children gave off a light, decadent fragrance. Pure starlight. It was as if the world had not touched them yet, not yet weighed down their blood. And she could make out another scent beneath the dried blood that reminded her of a fresh snowfall. Of midnight air and leather. Unfamiliar earth.

Where had Genevieve dragged him from?

Colette repeated in a whisper, "What have you done, Genevieve?"

"I found him." Genevieve's voice was strained, swelled with pride. It took a moment for the meaning to sink in. *Him.* As though it was a child she'd known all her life.

"*Everyone out,*" Colette roared, addressing the entire room.

The music cut off. Marie and Alice had stopped dancing already; they were staring at Genevieve. When Colette's fierce glare landed on them, they burst into motion, splitting off to herd every guest out of the manor.

Air swirled behind Colette, and she turned to find Giselle walking towards her. "What's happening?"

"You need to leave."

Giselle stopped short, her fingers raising to fix the buttons on her blouse. "But, you said—"

Marie walked past them, her arms hooked under two

giggling women. Her eyes flicked between Colette and Giselle, curiosity piquing her brows. And then she was gone.

But her presence remained, weighing on Colette's shoulders.

Colette's heart dipped, her stomach swirling with regret. "I know what I said," she bit out. "I don't need you to remind me. I'm simply not interested anymore."

Giselle's eyes shuttered. "All right…"

But Colette didn't let her walk away. Not yet. She gripped Giselle's upper arms and pulled her close, anchoring her eyes in those pits of hearth-fire brown. Giselle's pupils dilated as she fell under Colette's influence.

"Go," Colette said firmly. She hid every speck of feeling, every shred of her humanity and aching tissue of her dead heart, and did what needed to be done. "When you get home, burn the sketches you've drawn of me and never come back here. Never think of me again."

The frail hope of companionship evaporated, slipping through Colette's fingers like ash. Leaving a stain to remind her of what she'd lost and what she would never have.

It took decades to meet someone that intrigued her enough to consider something more permanent than a night or two, to meet a human who might have made her a little bit happy for a little while. But then Genevieve showed up and popped the bubble.

Marie had looked at her, and she felt everything inside her body shrivel up.

Giselle couldn't be allowed to remember, not with this child showing up. This went beyond sex and blood lust. *This* was unforgivable.

And Giselle couldn't be allowed to return either. To paint any of them, to immortalize all of their sins with her art. It was too much of a risk. Colette saw things clearly now.

Better to cut every tie, to be callous and brusque, to make Giselle feel as unwanted as possible. It would ensure she never came back, just in case Giselle's deep fascination for her managed to slip past Colette's enthrallment. Enthrallment was delicate, after all. Whatever Colette and the other women had become could plant seeds of will and thought. They could compel immediate action, but that power slowly deteriorated over time. Humans couldn't remember the sordid details of what they were told to forget. The women would have been burned at the stake by now if that was the case. But humans did remember the way those fuzzy memories made them feel.

For most, it was bliss.

For Giselle, it needed to feel like this.

Colette lifted her chin as Giselle blinked the daze away. The woman gave her one last lingering look and walked herself out of the room. When she was gone, Colette filled her lungs so full that it hurt, and turned to face the evil in the room.

She approached the couch that Genevieve had settled into.

The boy sat quietly beside her, his eyes on Marie. Marie had crouched at his side, a platter of fruit and cheese in her hands. The boy ate from it ravenously. Juice dribbled from his mouth as he ate the grapes, cluster by cluster.

Colette didn't want to know how long they had been traveling, how long he'd starved.

This was perhaps the closest a human could get to what they were, the hunger they felt. But a boy like this, so innocent, a reminder of what they had lost and sometimes longed for, should not have to feel like that.

Marie spoke softly. She said the same thing over and over, in various tongues, both common and rarer languages. He did not respond to any of them.

Alice closed the doors to the rest of the manor and leaned back against them to watch the others in the center of the room. Colette understood that she was guarding the exit.

Genevieve's hand tightened on the boy as she watched Marie try to communicate with him, his little fingers turning yellow and white from the loss of blood flow. Colette was surprised she had let Marie get so close in the first place. She was nothing more than a wild, madness-addled animal. She was too sick, and they all knew it.

Colette asked herself then, if they should have spared her before it came to this, if they should have put her down a long time ago.

Marie noted Genevieve's nervousness and said gently, "Viv, I won't hurt him. I swear it."

Genevieve's hold loosened on the boy's wrist, but not by much.

Out of the four of them, the connection that formed between Marie and Genevieve had been most surprising. Marie saw something in her that didn't really exist, had developed a tenderness for the quiet sharpness of Genevieve's presence. There was an atmosphere to the room that appeared every time Genevieve entered it, as though the shadows in every corner of the room were darker, as if they were *alive*.

Marie didn't shy from it, though. She felt a certain kindredness to her.

Colette couldn't understand why. And after what the

woman had let her spirits convince her of this time, she didn't want to.

Colette's eyes narrowed in on that bony little wrist. She could imagine the red ring around it, the mark of a shackle that did not belong there. It made her see red. It had her growling, "Let him go, Genevieve."

"I can't," Genevieve replied, her eyes welling with blood. "He hasn't been listening to me. He keeps trying to run off."

Alice muttered from across the room, "Enthrall him, then."

"No," Genevieve snapped. "No one touches his mind. It's fragile. The stored memories could be tainted."

That confirmed it then—who she thought he was. Colette almost felt sorry for her.

Marie understood then as well. She fronted a grim, reassuring smile and turned back to the child, continuing her attempts with more obscure languages, some even Colette did not recognize.

Marie had become intensely studious in immortality. Colette knew without asking that it was because she had been allowed to learn so little as a mortal, and felt she had a lot to prove to herself. Her hunger for knowledge rivaled even her hunger for blood, and she spent most of her time satiating one or the other.

"Genevieve, I'd like a word." Colette gestured to the open balcony doors.

Genevieve's back turned ramrod straight, her hand tightening once more on the child's wrist. She leaned over him. The boy stiffened as he marked the movement.

Marie spoke again, using a soft, compassionate tone that

Colette had not heard from her in decades. "I'll sit with him," she offered.

Genevieve opened her mouth as if to protest, but Colette stepped even closer.

"*A word.*" Colette willed her figure to loom tall and her authority to burn bright. Even after all these years, she managed to find a kernel of her previous self. The Lady.

Genevieve, on the other hand, had abandoned who she once was, stripped it off like a second skin.

It became clear to Colette decades ago that another sort of beast lurked in Genevieve's body, one that subsisted through her human life and whose manifestations were heavily veiled. Impalpable, like those invisible, whispering spirits. Colette was beginning to understand that some beasts knew what it meant to be human and could conceal themselves better than the ones that simply thirsted for blood. There were a few out there, like the one Genevieve carried, that actually fooled themselves into believing they were human.

Colette thought she glimpsed that strange other slithering beneath the surface, tapping from the inside of its fleshy mask as Genevieve met her stare, as she stood and followed her to the balcony.

In the open air, Colette put her back to the half-shut balcony doors and said, "Your son is dead, Genevieve."

"He was."

"Your son died forty years ago on the floor of my parlor."

"Forty-three years and ten days," she amended, rubbing the tips of her fingers together, as if at a loss for sensation. "I've been waiting patiently for him to return."

Colette nearly felt pity for Genevieve again, but it was

overshadowed by her irritation, by her fury. "What's dead is gone. He can't come back."

"*We* did. We should have died but we didn't. Death is only a temporary mantle. Those like us only carry it for a time, and then we are pulled back to the earth. The spirits told me so."

"And what else did they tell you?" Colette hissed. "To steal a small child away from his family? To starve him to the brink of death or suck him dry?"

Genevieve's eyes darkened. "I would *never* do that. I'm his family. I promised never to hurt him again if he came back to me, and I meant it."

Colette shook her head. "I don't care what your spirits have told you. That boy in there is not your son. Your boy didn't turn like us. He died mortal and went wherever mortals go. To paradise, to Light—paint human eternity with whatever brilliant colors will comfort you. But this deception *cannot* go on."

Genevieve's brow furrowed, a faint thread of doubt crossing her face. But then her chin twitched to the side, an almost imperceptible response to something behind her. "No," she murmured. "He had something in his blood that made him different. The spirits of the earth took him. They reanimated his soul."

Colette scoffed and turned to leave. "You've gone completely mad. We're going to make this right, right now."

But Genevieve caught her by the arm, twisted it just enough to hurt as she leaned in to growl, "Say that to my face."

Colette's green eyes met Genevieve's icy blue, their wills clashing like waves in a stormy sea. And Colette forgot to be afraid.

She threw her other arm out, down between them to break Genevieve's grip. Then Colette seized Genevieve's neck. Genevieve shoved back, snarling, and suddenly they were careening through the balcony doors, the wood splintering as they tumbled into the room and sprawled on the marble floor.

Colette had the upper hand.

Genevieve's measly diet of woodland animals made her skittish, too slender, lacking the nutrients she really needed. It was hardly a struggle at all for Colette to pin the woman beneath her, to straddle her legs and unsheathe the dagger from the folds of her sheer nightdress. Tonight, she finally found a use for it.

Beasts could be beheaded.

They'd discovered this from one of Alice's manic leaps from a cliff. She'd jumped simply to see if she could and had decapitated herself on the rocky crag below. The beast within her survived, but not in any way that mattered… not until they put the pieces back together.

Colette pressed the blade against Genevieve's neck, bracing her other hand on the woman's sternum. She breathed heavily, rage infesting her every muscle, her vision sparkling with shadow and red hot embers. "You've lost your *goddamn mind.*"

Genevieve bared her teeth, but she didn't fight back. Bloody tears streaked down her temples into those sprawling dark curls.

"You're going to return the boy to his home or tell us where you stole him from so we can. If you refuse, if you fight, if you try to run off, I'll break you into pieces and bury you in a dozen unmarked graves. We'll see exactly how useful your spirits are then."

The snarl faded to a sick smile as Genevieve leaned up into the blade until it broke her skin, until blood dribbled down her neck and pooled in the hollow of her throat. "You have no idea how useful they are."

A tremor rattled through Colette's spine.

Just when she made the decision to follow through on the threat, to sever Genevieve's neck and be done with this nightmare, something seized the muscles in her hand. An invisible hand wrapped around her fist to hold it in place, taking control of the knife.

Genevieve laughed, triumph glittering through the air between them as she said, "But you're about to find out."

Colette's arms shook as that invisible force raised them. She trembled from the effort of fighting back against whatever was touching her, but she was helpless. She couldn't move an inch in any direction. Her arm halted level with the ground, both hands gripping the handle of her dagger.

She glanced past the dagger and saw the others. Alice took the struggle in with round eyes, her body leaning forward as if trying to remember how to walk. Marie was still on the couch, her arms reaching out to pull the boy to her chest and quickly covering his eyes and ears.

"You forgot," Genevieve growled, not bothering to wiggle herself free. As if she wanted to feel Colette's blood spray all over her. As if she had dreamed of bathing in it for a long time. "What happened to us, what happened to him, still matters. There is a debt to be paid. If you will not allow me to make it right, you must be put away."

With a snap, Colette's wrists broke and curved in, towards her own chest. The tip of dagger pointed straight at her heart.

It may not pump the way it used to, but puncturing the

organ would still result in a loss of blood and consciousness. Even in death, a heart took longer to heal than the rest of the body.

Against her will, Colette's arms stretched outward, readying for the plunge.

Alice cried out, her limbs finally breaking free of their paralysis. The pressure around Colette's hands lessened as Alice rushed toward them.

But then, suddenly, Alice wasn't running anymore. She was lifted into the air. Something had wrapped their invisible tendrils around her neck. Alice clawed at her neck, grasping at nothing, scratching only her own skin. Her legs kicked, yearning for solid ground.

"Stop it, Viv," Marie begged. "*Please.*"

She didn't stand from the chaise though, torn between the young boy in her arms and her lover suffocating across the room.

They all watched as Alice's throat crimped like a dent in some metal and her limbs went limp. Then, whatever was holding her up flung her away like an inanimate doll.

Colette could see the end so clearly as the pressure returned to her arms.

If they all fell into an undead sleep, no one could guard against the dawn. The sun would come, filling this room and consuming their bodies with it's scorching light. There would be nothing left but ash, and their beasts would go wherever non-mortals spend eternity. She could not paint it in a way that comforted her.

The blade hurtled for her chest. Millimeters from impact, a hand speared into her vision and squeezed her broken wrist. Halting the blade. Her bones ached, but she breathed a sigh of relief when she looked up and saw Marie kneeling there.

The boy clung to her torso, his little fingers digging into her shoulders hard enough to leave crescents in her skin.

Marie addressed Genevieve with a shaky voice. "Viv, stop this. Colette can't see things as clearly as we can, she struggles with the truth. You know this."

Colette nearly let that dagger plunge into her heart after hearing that. It would have hurt less than the words Marie spoke. But then she saw the slight stretch of Marie's skin, the way her ears flexed back in the way they always did when she lied.

And Colette was forced to resign herself to a role she had little experience in—the one being rescued.

Marie went on, "She doesn't believe you. But I do. If anyone is to blame for the night we turned, it's me. I'm the reason you were there. It's my debt to repay. I'll help you with Julien, and we can leave the city together, just the three of us. Just no more of this. No more pain, *please*."

Genevieve stopped breathing, holding in all that rage and sadness, all that sickness. The shadows had multiplied around her face, far darker than they should be. They had buried themselves in her black curls and creeped up like hands crawling up out of the earth. But as Genevieve set her eyes on Marie, they retracted, lessened.

The pressure on Colette's limbs evaporated, and the world grew brighter as she realized that the darkness had pressed in on her too, like a mist. A darkness she couldn't quite see.

"Let them live without faith," Marie said softly. "Just let them live."

The dagger slipped from Colette's fingers, the muscles

and nerves of her crushed hand finally falling limp. Already she felt them trying to mend. A warm tingle spread through her tissues as her damned blood rushed in and soothed the hurt.

Marie pushed Colette away without looking at her, a gentle nudge that suggested she should back off, stand up. So she did.

She shuffled back, nearly tripping over the remnants of the balcony door as she inched out into the moonlight. Just far enough to feel the open air against the nape of her neck. Then she watched as Marie helped Genevieve to her feet, the small boy still attached to her waist.

Marie walked to where Alice lay.

She set down the boy on his own two feet and told him not to fear, that she was there with him and wouldn't leave him alone. Then Marie knelt beside Alice and kissed her pale, unresponsive lips. A goodbye. The only one she had time for.

Marie reached for the little boy's hand.

And in that split second, Marie looked at Colette. Their eyes met, and Colette understood. The calm on Marie's face ebbed, the true terror of what happened tonight passing between them like a strike of lightning. The truth was there and then it wasn't, sinking back beneath the surface like a beast.

Marie smiled slightly, then turned to where Genevieve waited—her figure a cloaked shadow at the entrance to the room.

All Marie had needed to say was conveyed in that instant. Her eyes had shone with love, as if to confirm that she indeed thought this was a return on some favor. As if she believed there was a debt to pay, just not to Genevieve.

But Colette wished Marie would have realized, through all of the love and rescues and friendship, she had not been keeping score. That, as far as the two of them went, what they shared was love without conditions. Love without regrets. Except for one, perhaps, after tonight.

She wished she had said all of that out loud.

ALICE

A steady drip drew Alice back to consciousness.

Drip. Drip. Drip.

Her head ached viciously, almost as much as her gums. She was starving. She'd lost blood somehow. As she tried to twist her neck, the entire length of her spine ground together as if compacted.

She remembered what happened then, the memories rushing into her mind like blood rushing to her injuries.

Genevieve came home with a child, and Colette had confronted her—a feat none of them had been brave enough to do before. Alice bolted upright, expecting to see the ballroom and the aftermath of Genevieve's anger, expecting to see blood dripping from the ceiling, but… she wasn't there.

She was surrounded by darkness.

The room was a landscape of grey and silver, but she could make out the familiar piles of dirty laundry. The stacks of wine. The set of four identical caskets lining the far end of the room. She was in the basement.

She tried to sort through her thoughts, but they all clustered together, disorienting her beyond words. Genevieve didn't kill them. But then, why wasn't she in her casket? Marie would have put her there… if she was able.

Slowly, Alice pushed herself up, leaning heavily on the side of her body that didn't feel stiff with healing.

Her eyes scoured the floor, hoping to see Marie lying behind her or some evidence that she was close-by. She found nothing. Her throat began swelling, and she knew it had nothing to do with her neck being snapped. Something had happened after she fell into hibernation. Something terrible. She felt it down in the pits of her heart. Her hands shook as they came together in front of her stomach, wringing and scoring. Her nails drew blood.

She could almost hear her mother's voice. *Don't pick, my darling. You'll ruin your pretty skin.*

But dreadful heat was filling her chest, overwhelming her nerves and driving her out of coherent thought. She rose to her knees and shuffled in a tight circle. Tears brimmed in her eyes, clouding her vision in crimson. That was how it felt all over her body. Bruised and broken. Pain in the empty darkness.

Except she wasn't alone.

Her eyes caught on movement in the corner. The roaring in her head stuttered, clearing enough to hear the sniffle. Alice put away her panic, covering it up the way she was so good at doing. She crawled forward, toward that figure, but didn't allow herself even a moment of hope. Alice knew it wouldn't be Marie.

As Alice's vision adjusted and the darkness parted, she saw Colette staring back at her. Her face was almost unrecognizable beneath the blood. She'd been crying for a very long time.

Alice ignored the dip in her stomach, the illness threatening to rise up out of her throat. "Where is she?"

Colette just barely managed to hold back her sobs. "She's gone. Genevieve took her."

Vision tunneling, Alice fisted her hands to keep from lashing out, from grabbing Colette and shaking the tears right out of her. She had no right to cry.

In a quiet but vicious voice, Alice said, "Why didn't you stop her?"

The accusation in Alice's voice quelled the tears.

Colette eyes narrowed, her upper lip curling. "I tried," she whispered. "But look at what she did to you. If I got in her way, we would both be ash under the dawn right now. Don't blame *me* for this."

"Oh, trust me," Alice said dryly, "I blame you for everything."

Colette recoiled. The meaning was clear—the accusation went beyond just this night.

"I know what I have done." Colette straightened her back, attempting to look down her nose at Alice. Little did she realize that Alice had not felt small in her presence for a long time, and she had no intention of returning to that place.

"If it wasn't for me," Colette hissed, "you'd be dead right now. You'd have been strangled in your brothel or murdered alongside Marie in that shitty little shack."

Alice scoffed. "I won't thank you for what you did to us."

Fire flashed in Colette's eyes. She struck the floor with her fists, snarling softly. "That's not what I want." And then something strange occurred. Colette's entire body softened, crumbled. She averted her gaze to the floor between them. Surrendering.

Alice had never seen her surrender before. It was surprising enough to convince her to keep any further venom to herself.

Colette trembled as she took a deep breath, and then she said, "I'm only asking that you not hate me right now, when we're all each other has. When Marie needs us."

There was no hidden hatred in those words. There was no animosity. It was a plea.

Alice wanted nothing more than to crush her in that moment. To take that tenderness, that vulnerability, and return every cleverly worded insult she'd made toward Alice over the years. It would be so easy.

But she was right.

Marie needed them.

Alice looked around the basement again. At their temporary refuge. And something sharp inside her dulled. She crawled forward, just enough for her to reach out and brush her fingertips against Colette's.

"I don't hate you. I can't."

Colette lifted her head to peer at Alice through blood-soaked lashes, saying nothing. It was too raw, too real, the way she looked at Alice in that moment. It made Alice feel as though all of her organs were shifting position.

Alice removed her touch and continued, "You saved me tonight, and we both know you didn't need to. You could have let me burn. But you did it for Marie. You saved me to spare her any hurt, despite the fact that your heart's desire relies on my death, and don't think I don't realize that."

Colette furrowed her brows. "What do you mean?"

Alice bit back a callous retort. Colette couldn't truly be this ignorant… could she? But as the silence stretched between them, Colette's expression didn't change. And that gentled Alice even further. Pity. It had to be pity she was feeling.

"You want her," Alice explained softly. "You might even love her."

"It isn't like that." The objection was too forceful, too immediate.

Alice smiled sadly. "You can lie to yourself as many times as you'd like, but you cannot lie to me. My heart can hear yours weeping."

Then Alice stood, before Colette could react. She walked to the bottom of the staircase and looked up at the sliver of light seeping in through the crack under the basement door. It was still early afternoon.

Air stirred, and she felt Colette settle into place beside her, shoulder to shoulder, looking up at that light. Another day, Alice might have pulled away. But she didn't this time.

"What are we going to do now?" Colette wondered aloud.

Alice cast her a brief glance, absorbing the helplessness on her face. The fear. The… love.

"We let them get a head start," Alice whispered before turning to her casket. "We'll allow Genevieve to think she got away. We'll let her guard fall, and then we come for them. We find our girl and bring her home."

PART III

THE END

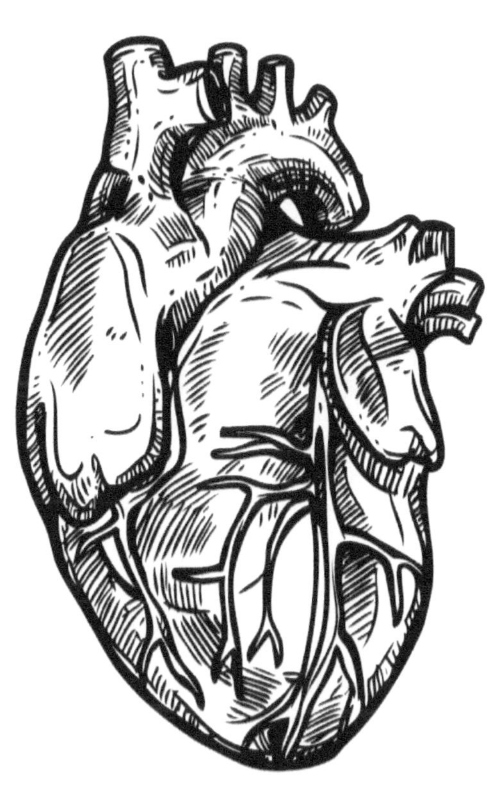

ALICE

16 years later

Alice strolled down the center of a dirt road, her eyes fixed straight ahead as the clopping grew louder. One set of hooves. She swallowed the venom in her mouth and kept walking, inching to the side of the road.

She let the rider decide their own fate.

The morning mists disturbed around her, swirling where it had once clung to her cold body.

As the hooves drew closer, they slowed to a walk. Then a deep voice said, "What's a pretty girl doing out here alone at this time of night?"

Alice craned her neck to look at the stranger.

He was older. Pale and slender, not a hint of hard work under his suit. Not one for labor, apparently. That was fine. There was something so satisfying about a soft, pliable body, untainted by muscle or adrenaline.

"I was just on my way home from visiting a friend. My

horse got spooked and ran off without me." That part was true, only she'd accidentally scared her horse off when she last fed. Animals were skittish when the *beasts* emerged. It was her own fault for not dragging her meal to a more secluded area beforehand. She wouldn't make that mistake again.

"I'm fairly certain I saw my horse head down this road. There's a town down the way, right?"

He nodded. "A mighty fine town, if I do say so myself."

"Your town?" she guessed.

"Indeed." His grin was a horrific, prideful thing.

Perhaps he had a little more to offer than blood, after all. Alice cocked her head, smiling sweetly. "Could you give me a ride?"

The man chuckled, his fingers tightening around the reins as he guided the horse closer to Alice. "I can, for a price."

Ah. So he'd made his decision.

"Oh," Alice sighed, pouting as though she didn't have a clue what he really wanted. "All of my coin is in the saddle bag, but I can pay you once we track down my horse?"

The man hummed, pursing his lips as he looked Alice up and down. "The town is quite a few miles out. How do I know you aren't tricking me for a free ride? What if you disappear on me the instant we get there?"

Alice didn't know how to disappear. If she did, she would have found Marie already. It's been far too many years, and she was so close now. Alice could feel Marie there, just beyond her fingertips.

"I suppose I can pay you right now," she said coyly, "but we should probably get off of the road for it."

A foul smile stretched his lips. "Of course."

Alice sauntered off the road, pausing at the edge of the trees lining the road to glance back at the man. After tying the horse to a tree trunk, he dismounted and followed her into the darkness.

"I think I've heard about Pesmes before," Alice said airily. "You have some of the best shops and your wares get sent all over the country."

"We do pride ourselves on our mastery of the arts."

"Especially the seamstress shops," she continued. "I've heard you have a real paragon living there, dressing your women in the finest styles this side of the country. Maybe I should order a dress for myself while I'm in the area. Do you know what time the tailor opens his doors?"

The man hesitated a moment, then said, "The best tailor in town runs his shop underneath his home. If you knock on his door when we get there, he should answer. He's an especially early riser. Unlocks the doors before dawn and closes a few hours after sunset."

"I'm not usually available during the day, so that's perfect."

Alice did her best to keep ahead of him, casting small smiles over her shoulder to keep him following her. Leading him further and further from the road. But he became impatient.

"I knew it the moment I laid eyes on you. You're one of those fancy, traveling whores, aren't you?" He grabbed her arm, and she didn't hesitate to shove him back against a tree.

Surprise and then anger flashed across his face. But Alice was good at soothing old men. She grazed her hands down his chest as she took a slow, measured step back.

"Guilty." She didn't specify how.

Alice knelt in front of him. "Now take off your pants."

"Eager thing, aren't you?" he drawled, reaching for his waist. "You want me in your mouth?"

More than you know, she thought. But she didn't say that out loud. She waited quietly, stoically, as he pulled off his pants and discarded them to the side.

Alice launched forward and pinned him to the tree. She sank her teeth into his thigh. The artery gushed, filling her mouth with his blood. It tasted like tobacco and cinnamon and burnt sugar. The man gasped and leaned forward, as if to push her away. But then her venom took effect. He groaned, sliding his hands into her hair, and she promptly snatched his wrists up and broke them. His cries were equal parts agony and pleasure.

Within minutes, the man collapsed. Empty. Bone dry.

Alice left the dead body behind in the trees, mounted the stallion, and rushed the rest of the way up the silent dirt road.

THE SHOP HAD the prettiest door in town. Yellow. And, granted, the paint was peeling in several spots, but it suited the quaint beauty of the town. Every street was lined with flower beds. Ribbons of all colors were tied around wooden beams. It was a town that blended the finest parts of both country and the city, which made sense considering how close it was to the capital.

Just the mountain pass and a river to cross.

The doorknob was cool to the touch, slightly wet from the fog as her fingertips found a dent on the underside. Alice opened the door and slipped inside. Bells hanging on the inside of the door jangled, announcing her presence.

A man sitting behind the counter on the other side of the room looked up, his hands lowering the ream of dark fabric he'd been working on. He was clothed in blue silk and ivory ruffles. His eye glasses rested low on his nose, rimmed in gold, the lenses slightly small for his face.

Four candles flickered on top of the table, swathing his work in bright light. He put the material down, pulling off his glasses and setting them aside with a smile.

"What can I do for you this morning, Miss?"

Alice strode across the room, hitching her overskirt to access the coin purse there. But instead of coin, she withdrew a torn bit of fabric. On the purple fabric, red thread stared back at her. An initial. An 'M' with the first peak crossed through the middle.

She hesitated in front of the counter, rubbing the satin between her fingers. Better than picking at her skin. She forced herself to return his smile. "Are you really the one who should be asking me that, good sir?"

His brows twitched downward. "Pardon?"

"I know your secret."

Firelight danced across his rosy-toned golden skin, the accompanying shadows dipping into the hollows of his cheeks as he grimaced. He didn't say a word. But he didn't need to— his concern was evident in the way his shoulders tensed, in the way he stood from the chair behind the counter. He was tall, *extremely* tall.

Alice placed the patch of fabric on the counter between them.

"You aren't the one making these dresses. I know this signature. Someone very important to me is here."

His dark, angular eyes narrowed as he crossed his arms tightly over his chest. "And who exactly do you believe that is?"

Alice's chest squeezed, every lick of her hope breaching the surface. She cradled them carefully in her mind. All the years she'd spent looking for evidence that her wife was still alive, the past five weeks she'd spent tracking down the maker of this particular dress, *all of it* came down to this. If Alice was wrong, she wasn't sure what she'd do. She couldn't go back to the beginning, to the endless unknown. Not again. "My wife. She's a woman about my height, has blonde hair and grey eyes. Incredible smile. Can you point me in the direction of where she lives? Is her home nearby?"

She didn't breathe as she waited for his response.

Recognition stirred in his eyes, but his body went still, as if he were telling himself not to move… not to give away the truth. He took his time studying her face.

Eventually, he averted his eyes and said, "I'm sorry."

Her stomach dropped. At first, she thought he meant she was mistaken, or that she'd been led to the wrong shop, or that it had all been a heart-breaking coincidence.

But then he continued, "I hope you understand the position I'm in. It would be despicable of me to betray the confidence of someone who works for me, whether you are who you say or not. As far as the world knows, you included, I'm the only one who makes our dresses."

Relief rushed into every limb of Alice's body, tingling in her cold skin. The refusal was as good as a confession. She huffed a sharp laugh. "I'm guessing that was her idea?"

But Alice knew it was.

Marie was more than comfortable being relegated to the background, while people like Colette and this fine gentleman socialized for her. In this case, Marie needed to send signs without alerting Genevieve to them. But she'd always been quiet and nervous and stunningly clever—quiet because she didn't know how to believe in herself, nervous because for the longest time, she thought of herself as stupid when that was the farthest thing from the truth.

Alice smiled weakly. Marie had found some faith in herself now, looking at what she'd accomplished in this town. Without the dresses, Alice wouldn't have found her way here. Marie had rescued *herself* with a needle and some thread.

"Does she come here often? If I were to wait in this shop, would I see her soon?"

Again, the tailor said nothing. He only chewed his lip and stared daggers over the counter, his fingers twitching against his arms as he kept them crossed. Alice got the feeling he was about to ask her to leave.

A commotion rattled the walls around her, and footsteps sounded suddenly from a staircase nearby, though she had difficulty pinpointing it.

"Mary!" a young voice shouted. "You're here early!"

Alice spun and found a girl standing in the doorway to a hidden staircase. She wore a simple white dress with lace and satin ribbons, and her black hair was parted in two long braids.

The little girl shrank back when she saw Alice's face, her eager smile evaporating. "Oh, you aren't my Mary."

My Mary. If Alice was unsure before, she had no doubt

now. Her wife had always had a way with children—they loved her. She could act so much like a child herself.

A genuine grin cracked her mouth open as she said, "No, I'm not. But it's okay, little one, you aren't the first person to mistake me for my wife."

There was one particular time that sprung to mind... but of course, she didn't like to think of that one. The one involving Colette and wine and a dark corridor just after they settled in the city. She'd laughed about it with Marie after-wards, but sometimes the details of that memory rose from the dead just to haunt her. This wasn't the time to let them in.

Colette was somewhere on the other side of the country, searching for Marie as viciously as Alice was. Alice should have retrieved her before coming here. They'd made promises to each other about finding Marie together. But the promises Alice made to her wife outweighed those. And maybe... maybe she'd acted a little bit out of selfishness too.

A petite woman appeared behind the young girl, filling out the rest of the doorway. Her eyes met Alice's, then flitted beyond her to the man behind the counter. Whatever the woman saw there made her reach out and grasp her daughter's shoulder. "Come back upstairs, Clover."

The tailor cleared his throat, and Alice twisted to look at him as his family retreated up the stairs and shut the camou-flaged door behind them.

"I think it's best if you go now," he said, the demand gentle but firm.

Alice didn't push her luck with the tailor. She didn't even attempt to enthrall him. There was no reason to. The child had told her all she needed to know.

Marie was to be here this morning.

Alice left the shop and walked a loop around to the backside of the building across the street. She waited there, between two of the wooden buildings, and watched the town wake up. It was still too early to worry about dawn. The sky was blackest night, speckled with hundreds and hundreds of stars. They hung heavy above her, reflecting the turmoil within.

Marie led her here with those merged initials, but Alice couldn't help but fear what would happen when they finally saw each other again. Had Marie missed Alice as much as Alice missed her? Why hadn't she come home or sent word before now? Over fifteen years of silence. The silence was so incredibly loud.

Alice tried to soothe herself by coming up with her own excuses, her own answers. But the reasons she believed the easiest didn't soothe her at all.

What if, when Alice finally did find Marie, she learned that Marie had not wanted to be found? What if all this time apart had only convinced Marie that Alice was totally, irrevocably broken and wholly insufficient? Alice's fears didn't align with what she knew of Marie, or the way Marie loved her… she knew that in her heart. But their hearts were also dead and rotting. So they couldn't really be trusted to endure the test of time, could they? Feelings changed, festered and dissolved, even the strongest of them. Hate. Love. It was all so inconsequential in the face of eternity.

Yes. Alice was frightened.

People started roaming the streets. Carts. Young men heading off to wherever they were needed. An old woman strolled by with her arms stacked with packages. And then, Alice saw her. The wispy, cloaked figure emerged from the fog, and Alice recognized her instantly. Her gait was the same. Light-footed and purposeful, a little like an animal on the cusp of spooking.

Alice took a step forward. Only that one. Because she was so frightened of being turned away. She watched, not even breathing, as that lithe figure approached the yellow door and slipped inside.

A few minutes later, Marie burst out of the shop and Alice jolted at the sight of her. Her lovely face, more beautiful than any memory. Marie removed her hood, exposing her golden curls and alarmed expression to the early morning blue. Her eyes scoured the street to either side of her. They danced across Alice's hiding place.

Alice flinched, retreating a step. It was absurd. She shouldn't be hiding. But her limbs were heavy and stiff, her chest tightening to the point of pain. Her eyes were trained on Marie, but she felt a thousand miles away.

She could only watch. Her mind was screaming at her to leave the alley and run to Marie, but her body refused to listen. And so she was stuck there, eyes burning as Marie's expression fell in what might have been disappointment. As she pulled her hood on and walked away down the street. It was only when Marie's face faded from view that Alice came back to herself.

Her fingers throbbed against her stomach, and she looked down to find that she'd picked her nail beds bloody. *You're going to ruin your pretty skin.*

Apparently, that wasn't the only thing Alice was capable of ruining.

Finally, Alice shook herself free from her doubt and left the alley, chasing after Marie up the street and into the woods.

She couldn't see Marie yet, but she felt her. Alice could *smell* her. So she followed that scent deeper into the woods, swatting away branches and leaping over logs. Alice was going to keep her promise, even if it hurt her in the end. Even if it made her insides melt and churn. The promise of forever, whatever that looked like.

She was scared of what might happen, but that was nothing compared to reality. Of losing Marie to her fears.

The trees went on and on, and Alice lost herself in them. Beyond the canopy, the sky was lightening to a brighter blue, signaling the coming sun. She should search for a place to hide. But Marie's scent was growing stronger, and Alice could not lose her. Not for another day. The days, which were so sacred to them. There was still no sign of her, but Alice kept chasing.

Just when Alice began to wonder if Marie had gotten away, the atmosphere shifted. A force collided with Alice and knocked her to the ground.

And that force. It remained there, on top of her.

"Alice?" Marie gasped.

Alice stared up into her wife's eyes, speechless, those depths of stormy blue-grey stealing all of her coherency. All she could think of were those lips, parted and trembling above her, billowing steam in the cool morning air.

Marie's eyes flitted across Alice's face, as if taking in every inch, every crease, every angle. Her hands bracketed Alice's wrists to either side of her head. She tried to speak, but the sound got caught in her throat. After a moment, she managed to get the words out. "It *is* you. He said you were there, but I, I couldn't—" Crimson tears tracked Marie's cheeks, dripping onto Alice's face and snapping her out of her daze. "You were there earlier—I felt you. Why didn't you show yourself before I went into the shop? After? I looked for you."

Though it became clear to Alice in that moment that she'd been wrong to indulge her worries, they fell from her tongue like rain. "I worried that you might have forgotten us."

Marie blinked, her mouth turning down at the corners. Her eyes anchored in Alice's.

Light to light. Fear to fear.

Marie's expression hardened with determination as she growled, "You can be so damn foolish sometimes." And then she crushed Alice's lips with her own.

With every slide of Marie's mouth, every tease of her tongue, Alice fell into an ache that felt equal parts familiar and new. Love. She'd missed feeling this love, spidering through her veins, filling her dead heart.

Marie wasn't being gentle. Her hands wrenched on Alice's skirt, frantically hitching the hem.

"What are you—"

Marie bit Alice's bottom lip, silencing her question as she shoved Alice's skirt above her navel. Her tongue dipped into Alice's mouth, capturing all the unspoken words. Marie slid her hand under the waistband of Alice's underwear. She caressed that tender spot right in the center, and Alice had never felt more alive than she did in that moment. Revived, really.

"You're going to accept the way that I love you," Marie swore. "Endlessly."

Alice moaned, her arms reaching up to twine around her wife's neck. Her beautiful wife.

Whatever brokenness Marie felt, it fit perfectly with

Alice's. They were carved from the same stone, two figures hewn into precious marble together. A celebration of form and intimacy. A heavy, hard love. And it would only shatter if she allowed something to tip them. So she wouldn't.

Alice lost control of her body. Her hips undulated under Marie's touch, riding her fingers, drinking from their pleasure. Marie shifted her body so that she straddled one of Alice's legs, and there was no hesitation, no pause to think about her actions as Alice drew her leg up between Marie's thighs. She threaded a hand into Marie's hair and gripped her hip with the other to encourage Marie to move.

"The day I forget you, Alice," Marie added breathlessly, "will be the day I die."

Pleasure coiled in Alice's stomach, spreading in sharp waves down into her toes. So close, but not quite close enough. She tightened her hold on Marie, thinking in her heart that she did not deserve it. Not after the horrible things she'd thought during their separation. Not after her doubt.

Marie slid her center along Alice's thigh, urged faster by Alice's guidance on her hip. She was soaking through the linen. She relished in the sensation. The slick heat. Warmth everywhere. It felt nearly as warm as being human.

Marie fluttered her touch lower, circling Alice's entrance before slowly sinking her fingers into that fiery chasm of velvet. There was nothing but sensation then. Nothing but friction and panting for air, whimpers and whispers of need. She felt a twinge in her wrist, a kiss of warning.

Morning was near.

Opening her eyes, she saw the sky shifting through the canopy of the forest. Strands of sunrise, of orange and magenta, spearing through the blue. But in front of that, she saw Marie looking down at her. So close to her own peak.

"I take it back," Marie choked out, her grey eyes searing into Alice, straight to her soul. "I would remember you, even in death. You are my heaven."

Alice's pleasure returned, rising swift and furiously until she was teetering on the edge. There would be no coming down. No retreating. There would only be the fall. And maybe Marie would fall with her, or maybe she wouldn't. But there was a faith there. Between them.

Alice drew her hands up to Marie's face, cradling her cheeks as she said, "I love you."

"Prove it to me, quickly, before the day comes," Marie taunted, smiling. "Burst for me, my love."

And Alice did. The world erupted with sparkling stars, burning and falling across her vision, spinning her into a dark nothingness. Where her mind was quiet and her worries were gone. Where her love was untouched by the brokenness she often felt so deeply. She was cleansed once again in Marie's cataclysmic fire.

MARIE

As much as Marie wished it could, their reunion didn't last. Less than half an hour after that moment in the forest, the sun drove them both into hiding. Alice found refuge in a nearby cave while Marie returned to the bunker. Because she had to return.

That little boy Genevieve stole had grown into a young man, clever and quiet, thoughtful. But he was also incredibly sheltered. He had not seen the world yet. He did not understand it.

And Marie had learned something great and terrible about herself over the last decade. She learned that she *loved* children. Loved being around them and playing with them, loved teaching them new things about the world and seeing wonder in their eyes. When she was mortal, children had always been such an acute point of contention for her, partially because her husband had expected children from her that she could not carry through his abuse, and partially because she'd been so frightened to pass her frailty on to them.

The boy became as much hers as he was Genevieve's. He made the time they spent in the bunker seem like a gift at times, because he showed her a type of love she didn't know existed before him. A love unconditional and pure. She learned to return that love selflessly, to grow it like a garden and eventually give it back to herself. It had healed deep, fissured parts of her.

Marie didn't want to leave him behind. She just hadn't figured out how to keep him yet.

If she simply grabbed him and left, they would face Genevieve's wrath. She spent too much time with her shadows. They seemed to become more a part of her than a part of the world, and at times, Marie was sure she could see them for herself, twirling through Genevieve's black curls and following her every step. The recesses of every room in their bunker had come alive. There was no way to know if the shadows watched for Genevieve even when she was away, to alert her the moment something went wrong.

Marie ruminated on that as she left the bunker this evening. Weeks had passed since Alice first found her. The seasons had changed since then, and snow fluttered from the sky as she navigated the woods, sticking to her cheeks like a thousand frozen kisses.

There wasn't a moment in the last couple months where she hadn't thought of leaving. Sneaking out of the bunker to meet with Alice like this, for only a few hours while Genevieve was doing whatever Genevieve did out in the world, wasn't enough. Marie was stuck in the same hell she'd been in as a mortal. Begging for moments of happiness, unable to possess love in its entirety. Longing for what was already hers.

She couldn't keep doing this.

As Marie ducked between two birches into a familiar clearing, she felt hands slide into place at her waist. Alice's body pressed into her back.

"Being away from you drives me crazy," Alice growled.

Marie smiled, resting in Alice's arms. "Good," she purred. "You love driving *me* crazy. This is repayment."

Alice made a face at that.

Marie laughed, twisting in the embrace so that they were facing each other. "What? You can't handle a return on your teasing?"

"Careful, my love." Alice said with a click of her tongue, grazing her fingertips across Marie's neck. "You're tempting me." She slid her hand into Marie's hair and pivoted them.

Marie fell back into the trunk of a tree and disturbed snow fell around them.

"To do what, exactly?" Marie asked around a smile.

"To make you come until you cry."

A shiver walked up Marie's spine, and it had nothing to do with the weather. "I don't believe you."

"You're beyond tempting, aren't you?" Alice whispered, her eyes burning into Marie, leaving behind a brand of love and desire. She stroked Marie's cheek with one knuckle. "You've become so brave."

Yes, she had. But she'd had no other choice.

The words struck Marie in her heart, never mind that it was dead. Life in the bunker was as dark and compact as the dirt it was cut out of, and yet Marie had never known any number of years as meaningful as these. Lonely, yes. Dismal even. But they were meaningful too—because of the boy. She grew to love him dearly, as she once loved her younger siblings in mortality.

Alice caught the shift in Marie's thoughts.

"I'm sorry, Marie. I shouldn't have—" Alice bit her lip, her eyes swimming with worry. "I don't pretend to know what you've been through after all this time."

Marie shook her head. "Let's not speak of it, not until I'm free of this nightmare."

"You could be free of it tonight if you wished."

"Alice."

She sighed. "I know. It's the boy, always the boy."

"He needs me."

After a moment's silence, Alice repeated, "I know." And then she said, "But I *do* have an idea, if you'll hear it."

Marie nodded. "Go on."

"I've been getting to know some sailors in the city. There's one Captain in particular, I don't think he would mind taking the boy on," Alice said in a rush. "Out there on the sea —how could Genevieve come after him? He'd be safe."

Marie turned the words in her head. "I don't know."

"Genevieve is still away. If we leave now, we could get him situated on a ship and out of the country ourselves before she even knows you're gone. We can run somewhere her shadows can't find us."

Marie squeezed her eyes shut, trying to hide her despondency. "You and I both know that's not possible, Alice. Shadows are our constant companions."

"Are you not even willing to try? Do you really think she would come after us?"

Marie's eyes fluttered open. She raised her hands to trace the braid along Alice's crown. "My heart says no, but I don't know what to think. She's gotten so much worse since you last saw her. More withdrawn. Unpredictable. I don't see the woman in her anymore, only her beast, and it terrifies me."

Anger flashed across Alice's face—anger and fear, but she quickly composed herself. She dipped her chin in acceptance. "We can wait as long as you want, my love, but you know it won't get any easier that way."

A faint snap sounded between the trees.

They both turned toward the source, a flicker of shadow in the distance. Without a word, Alice took off in a run, Marie on her heels. If there was one human quality immortality magnified more in Alice than the rest of them, it was her gracefulness—she weaved through the woods with ease, catching up to the retreating figure in a matter of seconds.

Marie barely made it to where Alice pinned the peeper down in enough time to stop her from sinking her teeth into the young man's neck.

"Alice, it's only Julien."

Genevieve's stolen treasure. He was as pale as the snow, his blue eyes fixed on Alice's canines. He knew from what little Marie explained to him over the years that they were capable of killing, and that they did it with their teeth.

Alice frowned but backed off, gripping Julien by the forearm to tug him to his feet. Then she moved to stand beside Marie.

Julien's eyes flicked between Marie and Alice, his jaw slackening.

"Julien," Marie breathed. "This is Alice, my wife."

He blinked a few times, slowly returning to himself. "Your wife," he echoed. "Since *when?*"

"Always," Alice replied tightly, tossing Marie a grimace.

An ache tingled in the back of Marie's throat. She knew what Alice must be thinking: why didn't Julien know about her already? Marie hadn't let her name fall from her lips once—not unless she was curled up in her bed alone, staring at the emptiness next to her. It was easier to not talk about Alice and the chasm separating them. To focus on surviving Genevieve and creating a home in the bunker for a little boy who needed one. The last fifteen years had been a nightmare, and nightmares did not allow visitation for pleasant memories.

"Forever," Marie added, trying to soothe the silent injury.

Alice averted her gaze back to the boy. She didn't show it outwardly, but Marie knew she was festering. Worrying.

"Why haven't we met before?" Julien asked. "Why don't you bring her to the bunker? It's so cold out here."

Marie smiled. "The cold doesn't bother us, dear."

"But it must bother you," Alice interjected crisply, folding her arms over her chest. "What are you doing out here? Spying on us? What have you seen?"

The insinuation prickled up Marie's spine. "*Alice.*"

Alice shrugged. "I'm just pointing out that he didn't seem prepared for introductions. He was peeping. I doubt this it the first time he's followed you."

"It's not," Julien conceded quietly.

Both women stared at him in surprise.

"But only this far," he added quickly. "I watch you two leave the clearing together, and then I return to the bunker. I swear it."

Alice scoffed at him, and Marie swore she saw a blush spread up his neck.

"I believe you, Julien," Marie said.

"Why don't you live in the bunker with us?" he wondered. "Living together is customary for marriage, isn't it?"

Alice answered, "Because if Genevieve knew I was here, she wouldn't be happy about it."

"Yes," Marie agreed. "It's crucial you don't tell her about this, about what you've seen here. Please."

Julien's brow furrowed. He contemplated that for a long moment. "Why?"

Alice curled her lip, a growl radiating out of her. Julien took a small step back.

"Just promise me, Julien," Marie insisted.

"Of course I won't tell her," he swore. "I promise."

Marie released a heavy breath. "Thank you."

Alice abruptly grabbed Marie's arm and pivoted them away from Julien, dropping her voice to a whisper as she said, "I think you should tell him."

Mare recoiled from the intensity in Alice's gaze. "I can't."

"He deserves to know."

"Know what, exactly?" Marie shook Alice's hand off her arm and did her best to ignore the hurt passing behind in Alice's eyes.

Marie was beyond relinquishing her will to anyone else. She knew better. Her true power lived within herself, as long as she had the confidence to use it, and she didn't need Alice to decide this for her, or guide her through it. This was more complicated than telling Julien the truth. Telling him could cause all sorts of untold damage, and without safety put into place for him, she had no way to protect him if he decided to leave them all behind. That was too real a possibility—his hatred. And Marie wouldn't blame him for it either.

"Shall I tell him that his entire life is a lie?" Marie

demanded. "That he might have had sunlight and a real family to love him if he hadn't been targeted by Genevieve and her shadows? Shall I tell him his true name, now that he has forgotten it? To what end?"

Alice pursed her lips, her features hardening as she finally replied, "To *the* end."

Yes. *The end.*

An end to the love and light that Julien had brought into Marie's life, an end to the intrinsic meaning and joy. It would be an end to his imprisonment, the suffering that he was not even fully aware of. Because no child was aware of the abuse they endured until it was past. And perhaps Marie had become a little concerned about how she would be remembered by him, concerned that the light she'd had would view her as a shadow.

But she suddenly saw that for what it was. It was time for her to let go, to forget her concerns. To put an end to all of it.

Marie spun to address Julien. "Go home, Julien."

He stood there, his body bundled but looking incredibly exposed anyway. The curiosity lingered in his eyes. The questions were still written on his face. "But—"

"I know you have questions, but they are not ones I can answer right now. Maybe when you're…older." The time was coming. He needed to go back to the bunker, where he would be safe until the right moment arrived.

Julien nodded as he dragged himself away, turning without a word and retreating through the trees. By the time his silhouette faded, Marie had turned away too. She walked toward town, her chest heaving with silent sobs, her tears staining her hands and the snow beneath her as the loss hit her in full. It was coming. The goodbye. And she was not ready.

Alice fell into step beside her, wrapping an arm around her waist and pulling her close. "Marie, what's going on?"

Marie closed her eyes and took a steadying breath. She took another and another, until she was calm and her resolve had solidified. Then she looked at Alice, admiring every angle of her face lit in the silvery moonlight as she whispered, "I think we need to meet with that Captain tonight, after all."

COLETTE

Colette galloped through the open gates of the estate, a full moon peaking in the sky above her. Winter snapped like teeth at her cheeks and lips and ears, but warmth curled in her chest when she saw the house appear at the end of the road. Home.

It had been a couple days since she last saw it, but at least this time, she was coming back with something of worth. Direction.

They'd moved to the outskirts of the city, into a cozy manor on an acre of field and farm. It was close enough to the sprawling center to host their lavish parties when they wished to, but far enough to take advantage of the privacy the land offered. The staff they now employed sufficed for feedings, especially since Colette and Alice were rarely at home anyway.

A stable boy ran from the barn and met Colette at the end of the lane.

She slid off her mare and handed him the reins. "Has Miss Alice returned yet?"

"Yes, and she arrived with a guest."

Thank the Light and all its stars. With Alice home, they could depart tonight. "Yes, very good. Thank you. Prepare a carriage for us; we'll be leaving again within the hour." She dismissed him with a wave and ran up the stone stairs to the front entrance.

The heavy door groaned as Colette pushed it open and slipped inside.

Colette had brought along all the decor from the great manor they left behind. It created a cluttered but warm aura in their new home, like a hug on the verge of suffocating. Velvet drapes and exquisite art on every wall, precious metal on every surface. Almost hazardous with all the candelabras lit throughout the house. It was… quainter than Colette was used to.

Marie would love it, once they brought her home.

Colette sloughed her coat and tossed it across an intricately hewn wooden bench in the entryway before continuing on into the greater belly of the house. The floors gleamed in the candlelight—so Alice had returned long enough ago that the maids started dusting and polishing again. She strode past the staircase and down the wide hallway that led into all the lower wings of the house. In the distance, she heard a hearth crackling, so she followed the sound into the drawing room.

Alice stood facing the fireplace, the light illuminating her haphazardly bound hair, her body angled over an open book in her arms.

Colette sauntered across the room with a smug smile.

"You can put that down now, my dear, and collect your things. Someone in the web has seen her."

The *web* was a string of minds Colette had spun for the sole purpose of finding Marie. All these years, and Marie was finally spotted a few towns North, in public. No telling exactly when. If they hurried, they might catch a trail.

But then Alice turned around, and all of Colette's plans drifted away like mist on water. Because it wasn't Alice.

Marie smiled, and it felt like the sun was there, shining just for Colette. "Is that right?" she teased. Hearing her voice made Colette want to weep. She was as beautiful as ever. Lovelier, in fact. She stood straighter, met Colette's gaze with a certain confidence that was new. Though, her disheveled appearance struck Colette as unusual.

"Marie." The word was a plea, a prayer.

Marie set her book down. "Yes, Colette. It's me."

Colette burst into motion, rushing across the room to gather Marie into an embrace. Marie's feet left the floor as Colette spun her and felt her laughing quietly as her arms wrapped around Colette's neck. Laughter might have bubbled up in her chest too, if she wasn't so overwhelmed with relief. Relief… and something else. An emotion so intense and sharp, it was almost painful. She had no name for it.

Whatever it was, it made her brave.

She set Marie back on her feet, then she took Marie's face between her hands and kissed her.

That emotion in Colette's chest grew thorns and teeth. It tore through every layer of flesh between them, every wall and barrier that had kept Colette from admitting the truth. She *was* capable of love because she loved Marie. Always had. Always would. Colette loved her for all that she was, and all that Marie brought out in her. Compassion and generosity and total vulnerability.

Marie stiffened, at first. But she didn't pull away.

Colette pressed in closer, breast to breast, her tongue tracing the seam of Marie's mouth. Marie gasped, and Colette was sorely tempted to find out if it was an invitation. But she didn't get the chance. A throat cleared across the room and Marie ripped herself away, her lips swollen and red as she turned to face Alice, who stood on the threshold of the drawing room.

Alice's face gave away nothing. No anger. No judgement. Not even a question in her eyes as she stared intently at Marie. "I'm sorry to interrupt, but I found something." She walked to a table in the corner of the room and spread a set of volumes out on the surface.

Marie pressed her lips together, avoiding Colette's gaze as she followed Alice to the table. Colette watched as Alice handed Marie one of the volumes and pointed out a particular passage.

Tension radiated from both of them, but it didn't seem to be connected to what Alice had walked in on. Colette glanced at the book Marie had been holding earlier. It was leather-bound, worn and yellow. They were searching historical records for something.

"What are you looking at?" Colette asked as she joined them at the table.

Without glancing at her, Marie answered, "A lead on where Juli—" She paused, closing her eyes briefly as if to recenter herself. "Where *Nikolai* might be."

Colette considered that, her brow furrowing. "Should I know who that is?"

"It's the boy Genevieve thought was her son," Alice explained quietly. "She found more of the flower to turn him, and then he ran away. We're trying to figure out where he might have gone so we can help him."

Ah, yes. Colette vaguely recalled that boy now. "I'm surprised Genevieve was careless enough to let him escape like that."

Marie looked up for only a moment, the truth written all over her face. Whatever had happened between them, Genevieve didn't survive.

Alice said quietly, "We never have to worry about her again."

"What happened?" Colette peered around them to look at the books on the table. The volumes were open to records about Northern European tribes. Farther North than Colette had ever dreamed of traveling. Interesting.

It was Alice who answered again. "Genevieve lost what was left of her mind. From what Nikolai told us before running off, we think she turned him because she believed it would unlock some buried memories that he was her son. That didn't happen. So Nikolai watched her burn in the dawn, and Marie barely saved him from burning with her."

"Nikolai was so upset," Marie whispered, her voice turning fierce. "We've been looking for him for close to a week now, but we're hitting dead end after dead end. I don't know what I'll do if something happened to him. Everything went so wrong so quickly. If we had just told him the truth—" Her voice broke.

"We'll find him, my love," Alice reached over and gently tucked a wild tendril of golden hair behind her ear.

Marie met Alice's tender gaze, a warmth seeming to pass between them.

But two words belatedly struck Colette. They wormed their way beneath her skin and dug a hole into her heart. "A week?" she muttered. "You've known where Marie is for a week now, and you didn't bother to send a letter?"

Alice looked at Colette. "It's been more than a week."

A tense pause. Colette swore she could hear her blood begin to boil. "How long?"

Marie recognized the gravity in Colette's voice. "What's happening?"

"I'm answering for a wrongdoing on my part," Alice said solemnly. "Don't worry, it doesn't concern you."

"*How long?*" Colette repeated.

"I found Marie in a town beyond the northern pass a few months ago."

The world vibrated around Colette as her fury became a physical ailment. "You've had her back for months?"

"Yes."

"How could you be so selfish after all this time," Colette snarled. "After the promises we made to each other?"

"I'm sorry." Alice grimaced, and maybe she was sorry. Maybe the guilt in her eyes was real. But Colette didn't care.

Colette pointed to the archway. "Get out of my sight. Get out of my house."

Marie's eyes rounded at the corners. "Colette, be reasonable."

And just like that, Colette anger pivoted. "She's been here since she found you. Did you know that?" she spat. "She slept in the room beside mine, fed with me, listened to me speak of you. I want more than anything to thrust my hand into her chest and rip her heart out so she can feel an ounce of what I feel. The betrayal. The disregard. Don't tell me to be *reasonable*."

Because there had been nights—those rare nights when they had laid down their differences and held each other to ease the loneliness. She and Alice. Their promises whispered under the covers, alone in the dark—promises of change and understanding. None of them survived the morning light.

What a terrible fool Colette had been to believe otherwise.

Marie's brows slanted inward. She absorbed everything Colette had to say, and then she nodded. "I understand why you're upset, but our hands were tied, Colette. We couldn't come home while Genevieve was still a threat."

"I didn't care about you coming home. I would have come to *you*. I would have helped you in whatever you needed." The anger split in Colette's voice, and all the softer truths oozed out. "Do you even realize how much I'm missed you, how deeply I've ached and worried over you? How much I *love* you?"

Marie smiled gently, reaching for Colette. "Well, I love you too."

"You don't understand." Colette shook her head sharply and staggered back a step. She looked away, trying to hold together the two sides of her chest that were presently cleaving apart. "You still don't get it. I love you beyond sense, beyond friendship, and I have not had a moment's peace since you went."

Silence followed. A deep, heavy silence, choking like black smoke. Colette dared to return her gaze to Marie and found her staring back with wide and glassy eyes, the gray in them swirling with surprise.

Colette continued, "I haven't been able to think of anything else. Only you, and what you must have been suffering. You should have put me out of my misery."

Marie pressed her lips together again, and in a less heartbreaking moment, Colette might have fooled herself into thinking it was in memory of their kiss. Just like she fooled herself into thinking Marie wanted it as much as she did.

"I didn't know—"

"Of course you didn't," Colette seethed. "The truth is that our relationship means nothing to you, it *is* nothing compared to what you have with Alice. You have your pretty, freakish whore to suckle and fuck you, so what use am I?"

Alice flinched.

It was as good as a slap to the face for how quickly it sobered Colette. Marie's own face hardened. She shook her head in disbelief as she turned to Alice and drew her into a comforting embrace.

Colette's chest wrested in half right then.

She raised a hand to cover her mouth, wishing she could take back everything that had just spilled out of it. The insults. The confession of her love. All of it. But that wasn't possible, so she did the only thing she could think of to make it right. She dropped to her knees and said, "I'm sorry. I didn't mean that."

Marie twisted to face Colette, pushing Alice behind her as if to shield her.

"Yes, you did. You always mean the horrible things you say." The woman who said that wasn't the *Marie* Colette remembered. This Marie… she was fierce and grim and fearless. Brutal. "And you know what's sad? I know you think even worse things about yourself, and you'll push everyone who matters away as long you believe them... so why should I bother coming home?"

With that, Marie stalked out of the room, leaving Colette to the mercy of her thoughts. She was right, of course. Colette's mind was her own worst enemy.

Marie's words lingered, devastating what was left of Colette's heart, and she found herself admiring Marie's courage, her raw strength and protectiveness. In that moment, Colette fell just a little bit more in love. And more into misery.

ALICE

Alice's heart was a rock in her throat. Her organs felt like they were dropping out of her abdomen one by one as she followed Marie outside. It felt like she was dying all over again. She didn't let herself show it, not as she witnessed Marie crumble right there on the veranda.

As soon as Marie hit the open air, she doubled over, bracing her hands on her knees. She struggled to get a deep breath around her gasps.

Alice placed a hand on Marie's back, and Marie stiffened under the comforting touch.

"I'm so sorry. I can't believe I—" she rasped, her body beginning to tremble. "I let her kiss me. I didn't mean to."

"I know," Alice whispered.

Marie lowered her knees to the ground and peered up with crimson streaking her cheeks, fisting Alice's skirt in her hands. "Forgive me."

And in that moment, Alice knew she already had. In fact, she'd been waiting for this day for decades, had known it was coming for them in the depths of her heart. She wasn't afraid anymore. Marie would never abandon her.

The feelings Colette had for Marie were as timeless and indestructible as their immortality. They would always exist. It was foolish to pretend she could ignore them, hoping they would simply fade over time.

No. They'd only grown, just as her own had, and it would be cruel to expect Marie to reject either of them. She returned those feelings, if not consciously then obliviously. And her love was great enough to envelop them both, if she wished. Alice had indeed lied and schemed, all in an attempt to keep Marie to herself for a little while longer, because she *knew* this was inevitable. She knew it from the moment she woke in that basement and saw Colette mourning in a corner. The thread that bound them all together was spun from diamond.

Alice sighed, cradling Marie's face in her hands as she crouched in front of her. "It's okay, my love."

"It's not," Marie sputtered. "She kissed me, and I didn't even realize that she—all this time…" she exhaled shakily, "and then she said what she said just to hurt us, to make us feel ashamed for loving each other. How could I let her come between us like that?"

Colette had been injured and afraid, like an animal backed into a corner. Her heart had been exposed to the elements. She'd lashed out to protect it. And no, that didn't excuse her intentions or what she'd said. But they'd all done terrible things, to others and to each other. Things that might have been considered unforgivable if they didn't have forever to dull the betrayal. Anger, after all, was only love misplaced. Jealousy, too.

"You didn't. Look at me, Marie." Alice nudged her chin,

and Marie met her gaze. There was so much confusion in her gray eyes, confusion and distress. "She's not between us."

Alice pressed her forehead to Marie's, and the tension weighing on them began to unravel. Marie reached up and clung to the sleeves of Alice's dress, and it all felt so familiar. So warm and right. But Alice hadn't said what needed to be said yet.

"I would understand if you loved her too," Alice added gently. "Or if you wanted to see if you could."

Marie's eyes snapped open, burning with offense. "Stop."

"I know you're angry with her right now," Alice continued, pausing to press a kiss to Marie's lips, to her nose and each of her cheeks, "but there's more beneath your hurt. You know it. I know it. And Colette definitely hopes for it."

The fury in Marie's eyes faltered. Her eyes slid shut again, a sharp breath rushing from her. After a long silence, she looked up and murmured toward the night sky, "Maybe, at some point in time, it might have been possible—the three of us. But I'm thinking maybe we missed it. Or maybe that point in time hasn't come yet, I don't know. All I know is that right now, I need peace." She dropped her chin and looked into Alice's eyes. "And you are my peace, Alice."

Whatever harsh, jagged edge was left in Alice's chest melted at that. She smiled and consumed Marie in a drugging kiss that went on for a small, blissful eternity. When she pulled away, she whispered. "You are mine."

Marie nodded weakly and asked, "Could you just make me forget the rest for a little while?"

They had an infinity together to figure out the rest. The complicated feelings. The young beast that had been let loose on the world. They had nothing but time to make it right again, now that there was no shadow hanging over them, no crumbling earth under their feet.

Alice started pulling the pins out of Marie's hair, letting her golden curls tumble down her back and gleam under the moonlight. "It would be an honor, my love."

COLETTE

Colette only allowed herself one minute to cry, and then she told herself to stop. She swallowed the lump in her throat and blinked away the crimson film. What would crying do for her now? She'd gone too far this time, and Marie made it clear there was no coming back from it.

Why should I bother coming home?

But she'd bought this house for Marie. She should have it.

Colette stood from the cold floor of the drawing room and silently glided through the halls and up the staircase to her room. All the windows in the manor were shuttered with custom wooden coverings that shut out every last trace of light, so Colette stood in that darkness for a while and brought herself under control. She cleared her mind and body until she started to emulate the shadows. Empty. Unknowable.

Then she lit a candle and got ready.

She donned her finest gown, a river of emerald satin and dripping ivory lace, and sat at her vanity. She wiped her face clean and drew kohl around her eyes to hide the rims of red, then painted her lips scarlet. No more tears. No more feeling. She went through the motions, and it reminded her of her human life. Back when she woke next to a husband she could not love and pretended there was happiness to be found despite her circumstances. She made herself numb because that was the only way to get through it.

Colette wished she could be numb again.

The truth was that her heart was as alive and aching as it had ever been, spoken for in a way she could never forget. She'd always worried she wouldn't know love, but that wasn't the problem. The problem was that she always ruined it.

She knew she was leaving her heart here, even as she packed her possessions away and had the staff load them onto the carriage waiting out front.

Colette didn't say goodbye because there was nothing good about it. She would leave them to their love and happiness, to their lightning and lust. She'd let her heart remain on the doorstep of the house, desiccating as it waited for a door that would never open. She should have known it would end like this for her: alone. That was what she'd prepared herself for by pushing away those that might love her, why she let her fear sharpen her tongue and draw more blood than her teeth ever did.

She simply wasn't designed for love.

As she approached the carriage, the stable boy opened the door for her and helped her inside the pitch black belly. Before he shut the door behind her, she handed him an envelope that held the deed to the house and asked him to deliver it to Marie after she was gone. There was no letter accompanying it. Nothing for Marie to despise.

The carriage was also customized with iron-clad wooden

panels on the windows. It was the perfect transportation for over-day trips, and there would be a few days in between here and her destination—a property she bought many years ago in the heart of the country. Far enough away that Marie would never have to see her again. It wasn't even close to dawn yet, though, so Colette removed the cover from the window beside her as they rolled up the drive.

The trees lining the lane grew thicker and thicker as they left the property and turned onto a public road leading away from the closest town. It was all forest from here to the larger cities in France.

Colette rested her head against the carriage wall, letting her body go limp as the dirt road jostled her about. It was strangely comforting, like being in a womb. She could pretend that she was about to be reborn, delivered to some new life where she had no need of a heart. No need of anyone but herself. Even as she thought it, she found it foolish. She had never been content in her own company. That was what all the parties were for, full of personality and noise and distraction. She knew it would be more of the same when she got to where she was going.

She was considering all the parties she would yet have when she saw something move in the trees just beyond the property. Something distinctly… inhuman.

Lurching forward, Colette banged on the front wall of the carriage and commanded the driver to stop. When he did, Colette departed from the cab and stared down the road at the spot she'd seen that flash of white and crimson. It had been a silhouette of a man, she was sure of it. And there was no other estate out here.

The driver turned to look at her. "What's the matter, my Lady?"

"My glove flew out the window," she said smoothly. "I just need to retrieve it. I'll be back."

She walked down the road, sticking to the shadows. Her footsteps were light and soundless, and the man she walked up on didn't even notice her as she spotted him between the trees.

He was tall and lean. His clothing was torn, a shirt and tunic sewn of the finest blues, and a pair of dirty leather trousers. He was barefoot in the snow. She saw the blood then, staining every inch of exposed skin. His hands were brown with it. It had dried in large splotches across the front of his trousers and tunic. Old stains. She couldn't even discern its particular scent anymore.

Colette ascertained several things at once.

The blood was not his own, and so he'd hurt someone. Multiple someones, even. Considering the blood dried on his neck and streaked through his hair, he had used his mouth to do at least some of the killing, and so she saw that he was a beast, like her. He was here, just outside their home, and so this must be the young man Marie was so worried about.

She emerged from her cover behind a tree. "Nikolai, I assume?"

He jumped, spinning to face her. His eyes flickered over her full figure as he asked, "Who are you?"

"My name is Colette. Don't be afraid, I'm Marie's—" The words caught in Colette's throat. What *was* she to them now?

"Her friend," Nikolai said on an exhale, nodding. "Yes, she mentioned you."

Colette's brows piqued. A small fleck of hope drifted through her. "She did?"

He chuckled without humor. "Of course. You turned her," he said dryly.

Her throat seemed to drop through her stomach as those words registered. She smiled to hide her disappointment. "I'm sensing some hostility surrounding that fact. Is your turn still a bit raw, Nikolai?"

"Somewhat," he bit out.

"Well, I can assure you, I'm nothing like Genevieve. I'd like to think I'm more of a dream than a nightmare, as long as you don't get on my bad side." Colette winked.

As teasing as it was, that comment seemed to soften Nikolai. He staggered back a step and ran a hand through his hair, glancing up at the sky and then toward the estate. He gestured vaguely in that direction. "I wasn't sure I'd be able to find my way here. But after I found—after what happened—everything blurs, really. I don't know how I made it."

"That's what we do." Colette shrugged. "You and I, what we are. We endure."

Nikolai peered at her from the corner of his eye, nodding gently. "I've been pacing here for hours, trying to get myself to go to her. To admit what I've done."

The possibility settled over Colette's shoulders. Looking at Nikolai, she saw a brokenness she had only seen once before… in Marie. It started as a sparkle in the darkest corner of her mind, illuminating the dark. Not love, but companionship.

Everything that had brought her to this point felt like a circle, with this moment completing it. Marie and Alice had each other. What did they need *him* for? This could be hers.

"You could walk up the road to Marie. It's not far now," Colette said, smirking faintly. "You could go to her and be coddled, be told it's not your fault, be comforted and cared for like the child you used to be."

His eyes narrowed, darkening at that.

Colette cocked her head, smiling. "Or," she drawled, "you could come with me and learn of your true nature without the sugary coating. You could leave with me and raise a little hell."

Nikolai blinked, dropping his gaze to study his blood-stained hands, as if looking for an answer in the muddy lines.

After a long moment, he raised his head and looked at Colette, his eyes as empty as the night around them. "Where are we going?"

THE END

Thank you for reading!
If you enjoyed this book, please consider leaving a review on
Amazon and Goodreads.

THE END IS ONLY THE BEGINNING…

Nikolai's story continues in Beneath the Bloody Aurora

Polar night.
Demon blood.
An undeniable attraction.

ACKNOWLEDGMENTS

The biggest thank you to my reader for taking a chance on me. You are amazing.

To my husband, thank you for accepting every part of me, for being the absolute best husband and father, and for reading my queer stories and telling me they are beautiful. I love you so much.

Thank you, Brittany, for your belief in me and for being a wealth of knowledge on my journey into self-pub. I appreciate you!

To my critique partner, Shannon: as always, you are a bright, shining light to my first drafts. Thank you for your endless encouragement, honesty, and jokes on the difficult days. I don't know what I would have done without you.

Thank you to all of the incredible writer/reader friends I've made online over the last three years. I never dreamed that I'd be able to find community, acceptance, and love from people I've never met face-to-face, but I did.

I found you all.

ABOUT THE AUTHOR

Beka Westrup is an emerging author of fantasy romances. Blood in the Tea Leaves is her second publication. She lives in Boise, Idaho with her husband and two sons, collecting more books than she'll ever be able to read and drinking copious amounts of iced coffee.

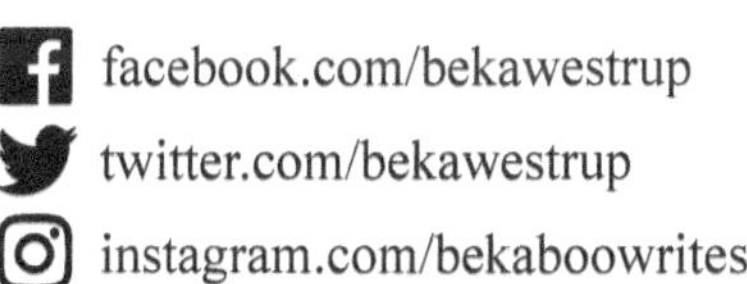

ALSO BY BEKA WESTRUP

Beneath the Bloody Aurora

The Seldom Wings (Summer 2023)

Song of Dark Tides (coming Nov 2023)